Christian Jr./Sr High
2100 Greenfield D
El Cajon, CA 920

DATE DUE

#47-0108 Peel Off Pressure Sensitive

THE POWERLINK CHRONICLES

TRUTH SLAYERS

THE BATTLE OF RIGHT FROM WRONG

A **NOVELPLUS** BY
JOSH McDOWELL & BOB HOSTETLER

WORD PUBLISHING
Dallas・London・Vancouver・Melbourne

Library of Congress Cataloging-in-Publication Data:

McDowell, Josh.

    The truth slayers: the battle of right from wrong/by Josh McDowell & Bob Hostetler.

p. cm.

    Novelization of message contained in adult-level, Right from wrong, by same authors.

    Summary: On a dig in Israel, teens from the youth group at the Westcastle Community Church grapple with various moral decisions, while several of Satan's underlings try their best to lead the teens astray. Includes sections that relate the story to real-life decisions and matters of spiritual growth.

    ISBN 0-8499-3662-4

    [1. Christian life—Fiction. 2. Conduct of life—Fiction. 3. Truth—Fiction.] I. Hostetler, Bob, 1958-   . II.

McDowell, Josh. Right from wrong. III. Title.

PZ7.M478446Tr 1995   94-47961
[Fic]—dc20   CIP
                                              AC

56789LBM 987654321

Printed in the United States of America

Table of Contents

Acknowledgements

We want to acknowledge the professional service of David N. Weiss in his creative development of the novel's story line. His insight and expertise guided us at every step as we molded the story into its final form. We are grateful to Alyse Lounsberry, editor at Word, Inc., for her valuable editing skills and preparing the manuscript for printing. And finally, our thanks to Dave Bellis, my (Josh) associate of seventeen years, for his creative design of the NovelPlus format, conceptualization of the initial story line, focusing the content and keeping it focused, rewriting and editing the many pages of this book, and overall directing the Right from Wrong Campaign, of which this book is a part.

Josh McDowell

Bob Hostetler

1

Wild Nights in Westcastle

Fifteen-year-old Brittney Marsh shivered in the dim lights of the Westcastle Mall garage. A light drizzle fell on the grass and bushes that lined the outside of the three-story garage, but it wasn't cold; it was late May, in fact. Only a few days were left in the school year.

She had come to the mall with her parents and had quickly made an excuse to get away from them. She had secretly arranged to meet someone in the mall garage, but she was already regretting that decision, not only because clots of cigarette-smoking teens in hooded jackets occasionally passed her and aimed crude comments in her direction, but also because she was beginning to think she had made a mistake.

She swallowed. Her deep brown eyes nervously searched the dark corners of the parking garage; her pretty pixie features twitched with worry and nervous energy. She tucked her shoulder-length brown hair behind her right ear and pondered her situation.

Part of her wanted to go through with it, but another part of her wanted to leave, to dash back into the mall, and join her parents before she made an awful mistake. She told herself to forget her clandestine meeting and do the smart thing, but her wildly beating heart urged her to go through with what she had planned.

Suddenly she froze. The headlights of a car lit the garage, and flashed her direction. She tried to peer beyond the light to determine if it was Matt's gray Pontiac Grand Am heading her direction, but the car spun its wheels before reaching her and headed up the ramp to the garage's upper level.

Brittney relaxed, no longer poised to run. She inhaled deeply, folded her arms on her chest, and remembered how things had started between her and Matt. He had asked her out the first week of school last September, two weeks after her fifteenth birthday; he was sixteen, and she was flattered by the attentions of the dark-haired junior who already had his driver's license.

Their first date wasn't even a real date. She told her mom that she was going to the Westcastle Library after school (which wasn't a lie; she just didn't mention she was going there with a boy). She and Matt studied in a remote corner of the huge library. Even though math was her best subject, she repeatedly asked him for help with her geometry homework, just for an excuse to talk to him, to feel him lean closer to her, to have him touch her hand or arm or shoulder. She smiled at his faltering explanations, and basked in the attention, which was something new to her.

She and Matt became closer every day, it seemed, after that. They spent every available moment together, and their relationship became more intense. Matt made her feel pretty, and important. She never had to ask her mother what true love felt like; she knew.

As her love for him grew, she began to yield more and more to his persistent pressure to become more physically involved. Initially, as a young Christian, she tried to resist Matt's ardent advances, but her hunger for love steadily wore down her convictions, until every date became a search for a dark, remote place. Within a couple months of their first date, Brittney and Matt's relationship had crossed every boundary; they were fully involved with each other sexually.

Physical involvement had not brought the emotional rewards she longed for, but had only increased her sense of loneliness and emptiness. She often determined to try to turn back the clock with Matt, to recapture those times, just a few months earlier, when they talked and did fun things together, when they were satisfied just to be in each other's company, when just the touch of his hand on her arm was thrilling. She tried, and failed. She and Matt seemed powerless to reverse the direction of their relationship.

So she ended it. She met him after school and walked with him to his car. She choked back tears as she explained everything to him, and ended by telling him that she had decided to break up with him.

His face paled as he listened. "Why?" he asked. "Why are you doing this?"

"I told you why," she said. She cradled her books against her chest with both arms.

"But I love you," he said. He stepped closer to her and dropped his voice. He locked gazes with her, and she saw that his eyes were ringed with red. "If we love each other, what's wrong with it?"

"I don't want to do those things anymore," she answered, darting her eyes quickly away from his.

Matt stepped back and spread his arms. "All right," he said. "All right, we don't have to. We can go back to the way things used to be, OK?"

"That's just it, Matt. We *can't* stop. We've tried, remember?"

"Yeah, but . . . we can try harder."

"It won't do any good."

He placed his hands on each of her shoulders and leaned his face close to hers.

"Don't, Matt," she said. Her lip quivered.

"I don't want to lose you," he whispered.

She shook her head. She had to get away from him, or she knew she would crumble into his arms. *It'll be easier when I'm not around him,* she told herself. She turned slowly and walked away, leaving Matt standing beside his gray Pontiac Grand Am.

That had been a couple weeks ago, and although she had never told him, her feelings for Matt hadn't diminished at all. They still talked, at school and sometimes on the phone. Matt had refused to give up. He never groveled, but he insisted that he loved her. And, while she never told him, she couldn't seem to stop thinking about him.

When her parents agreed to go shopping at the Westcastle Mall Saturday night, Brittney had immediately called Matt and arranged to meet him. *I'll just tell him we need to talk*, she thought. *Maybe this time apart has been good for us. Maybe we can start over.*

Now, however, as she stood on the curb in the mall's dingy garage, she shivered with emotion. She knew that she and Matt would slide into the same patterns as before; she knew that neither would be able to say no to the other, that their relationship would lead to the same kinds of behaviors and feelings as before. She was miserable without Matt, but she remembered how dirty and guilt-ridden she felt when she was with him.

She heard the roar of a car engine. She lifted her gaze to the garage entrance, and squinted into the headlights of another car. She knew it was Matt when she saw the front headlight jiggle as the car ran over a speed bump.

She hesitated, covered her mouth with one hand, then turned and ran crying back into the mall.

Brittney rounded the corner by the Zork's Castle video arcade and heard someone call her name. She turned, lifted her gaze, and screamed. She covered her mouth with both hands and stumbled backward.

Jason Withers stood outside the arcade, smiling.

Brittney let out another short scream. "What happened?" she asked in a thin voice, pointing to Jason's bald head.

"Do you like it?"

She withdrew her hand and quickly wiped her eyes, hoping Jason wouldn't say anything about her tearful, trembling expression when she bumped into him. "What happened to your hair?" she said. Her eyes flitted from Jason's clear blue eyes to his once-blond head.

"I was kind of giving Todd Marcum a hard time at the beginning of the season," he said, referring to the shortstop for the Eisenhower High baseball team, the Generals, "because they had such a bad year last year." He grinned sheepishly. "I promised him that if the Generals won the division, I'd shave my head."

"You didn't!" Brittney laughed, and covered her mouth with her hand again. "It just looks so . . . so weird." She stared at his bald head as if reading a message written there in fine print.

"Wow, thanks," he answered sarcastically.

"You know what I mean." She lowered her gaze and twirled a gold bracelet around her wrist. Jason flashed an apprising glance at Brittney, admiring her fine facial features and petite feminine form. He kicked himself inwardly for being the kind of guy who would shave his head and prompt giggles from pretty girls. He knew that he wasn't drop-dead handsome, but he considered himself a fairly good-looking guy: five-feet-nine inches tall with no scars, boils, or oozing sores. His problem, he knew, was that he was always goofing off; girls never took him seriously. They seemed to think of him as a fun guy, even a big brother sometimes, but never as a potential prom date.

Brittney's eyes suddenly widened and she looked up again. "What did your parents say?"

Jason's face reddened. "My mom never told me, but we were supposed to get our family pictures taken this Saturday. When she saw this," he pointed to his head, "she went ballistic." He lowered his voice and adopted a serious tone. "She actually cried," he said. "I felt really bad."

"Are you grounded or anything?"

He shook his head. "But Mom had to cancel the pictures."

She shook her head. "You're so funny, Jason."

He cringed inwardly and searched for a way to change the subject. Suddenly his eyes widened. "Oh," he said, "did you hear about Shane Richardson?"

Brittney recognized the name. She didn't really know Shane, but he was in one of her classes at school. She shook her head.

"Will told me he's dead," Jason said, referring to his best friend, Will McConnell, from whom he'd heard the news that afternoon. "He was shot. At a party at Tom Matthews' house."

Brittney's mouth dropped.

Jason shrugged. "I guess he and Tom were playing around with a gun and it went off."

They faced each other in silence for a few moments. "I didn't really know Shane too well," Brittney said finally, her voice flat.

"Me neither. Still . . . "

"Yeah," she agreed.

The conversation faltered again. Brittney spun her bracelet around her wrist as they chatted; her thoughts returned to Matt. She looked toward the doors to the garage area beyond the arcade. He had not come into the mall since she'd stood there talking to Jason. She wondered if he was still out there, waiting in his car.

Jason surreptitiously admired Brittney as they faced each other, carefully averting his eyes whenever she lifted her eyes. He knew of Brittney's break-up with Matt—the whole school knew—and he wished he could find a way to step into the vacancy. But he found it impossible to let Brittney know how he felt. Though Jason Withers seemed to have a million friends, and many of them seemed comfortable confiding in him, he had always hidden behind his jokes and pranks, never confiding in anyone himself, never letting anyone see the real Jason. But that would all change, he had decided, by the time he got back from the church youth group's summer mission trip to Israel.

"Hey," he said suddenly, snapping his fingers. "Have you thought any more about going to Israel with us? It's going to be really cool, you know, working on a real archaeological dig, thousands of miles away from home, in a foreign country."

She looked at Jason with sudden surprise. "Yeah," she answered. The thought turned around in her head to the accompaniment of the blipping and beeping music of the arcade. *That may be just what I need*, she thought. Her lingering love for Matt was driving her crazy and she knew he wouldn't give up until they were back together, and in the same old patterns as before. The mission trip was six weeks long; that should be enough time to help clear her head and maybe get Matt out of her system.

"Yeah," she repeated to Jason. "I think that's a great idea. What do I have to do?"

James Milford, the pastor of Westcastle Community Church, closed the front door behind the departing police officer and wheeled to face his wife and son.

Seventeen-year-old Philip Milford sat alone in the overstuffed chair opposite the couch. His mother stood in the doorway between the living room and the kitchen; she stared at the floor, looking at neither her husband nor her son.

"You were at that party," the pastor began, his face nearly purple with the emotion he had stored during Philip's interview with the polite policeman. The officer had arrived at the Milford home Monday afternoon, explaining that he had to ask some further questions of everyone who had been at the party in which Shane had been killed. He had spoken to Philip for about twenty minutes, asking for more details about what Philip had seen and heard, where Tom had gotten the pistol, and who else had been at the party.

Philip had arrived home late Saturday night, but his parents had been later still. When he remembered that his nine-year-old sister was sleeping at a friend's house and his parents would be returning late from an evangelistic crusade several hours from home, he went to bed relieved that he would not have to tell his father about the tragic events at Tom's house. His sleep had been filled the last two nights with gruesome memories of the party, the shooting, and Shane's bloody corpse, but he had avoided a scene with his parents.

"You were at that party," the pastor repeated. It was not a question. "Where that boy got shot."

Philip shifted his position and draped a leg carelessly over one arm of the chair. He had endured many of his father's lectures, especially about the friends he chose. He sighed loudly, convinced that this would be one of the worst.

"Dad," Philip moaned. He rolled his eyes at his father. "Look, I barely knew those guys."

"Then what were you doing at their party? Why are you even hanging around with those kinds of people?" He shouted the words, his arms flailing the air like unmanned fire hoses.

Philip knew what was coming next. He leaned his head against the back of the chair and closed his eyes. His father launched into an impassioned denunciation of Bobby Moses, Bo Shiffman, and the rest of the crowd that Philip hung around at school. In recent months, Pastor Milford had become even more expressive about Philip's "perilous" friendships.

"You see what happens when you choose those kinds of friends, don't you?" Pastor Milford was saying. "You see the trouble that follows guys like that? How many times have we talked to you about that, huh? How many times have we talked to you about that crowd you've been hanging around with?"

"You haven't talked to me about *anything!* You never talk. All you ever do is yell!" Philip stood, his face red with anger.

"That's because it doesn't do any good to talk to you. I can talk 'til I'm blue in the face and never crack that thick skull of yours!"

Mrs. Milford spoke the pastor's name softly, but he ignored her. "I'm done trying to get through to you, Philip. I'm through talking. It's time for me to take action, and that's just what I'm going to do." He shot a glance at his wife, as if looking for support for the decision he had just made in that instant. He turned quickly back to face his son. "You're going on that summer mission trip," he said, slowly and firmly. "With the church youth group."

"No!" Philip shouted. He had big plans for the summer, including a job he'd lined up at a local radio station; his father was ruining everything.

Pastor Milford held up his hand like a traffic cop stopping traffic when Philip opened his mouth to speak. "It'll do you no good to argue with me, young man."

Philip's mouth snapped shut, and his face grew redder. He stormed from the room, stomped down the hall, and slammed his bedroom door.

The Milfords stood in silence for a few moments. Finally, the pastor lifted his head and looked at his wife.

"I know," he said, "I did it again. I just keep thinking, if we could just get him away from those friends of his . . . "

☆　☆　☆

Far below Westcastle, deep within a maze of subterranean caverns and canyons, a lone figure hunched in a dark passageway beside a thick gray door. Like all demons of hell, the creature possessed an ugly mutant body—a cruel, mirthless joke perpetrated by Satan on the angels who had rebelled with him and so lost their lofty heavenly positions.

The demon, whose name was Ratsbane, inhabited the warted body of a giant toad, topped with the magnified head of a carpenter ant. His bulbous eyes reflected his surroundings like convex mirrors made of obsidian. He moved with an awkward, halting gait caused by the great difficulty he always had, coordinating his mismatched body and head.

Ratsbane fingered the coarse paper he held in his hands. The directive announced his deliverance from drudge duty, and his appointment to the vaunted Research and Intelligence Division. He reread the message assigning him to assist Maury, the famed demon genius in charge of the Research and Intelligence Division.

He opened the door and entered another long hallway. At the end, a coiled serpent guarded a door painted with the initials RAID. Ratsbane identified himself curtly to the serpentine guard, who read the directive as Ratsbane held it out before him. Then the guard hissed out directions to the demon Maury's lab.

Ratsbane waddled down a dim hallway, past door after door on both sides. The doors were labeled with cryptic assortments of letters: CMP SX, SBSTNC DVP, VRTL RLTY, ALT RELNS, and so on. He turned a corner at the end of the corridor, and immediately found himself on a steel balcony overlooking a large room swarming with so much frantic activity that it resembled the floor of the New York Stock Exchange. Whirring machines, ringing telephones, and flashing monitors dotted the room; demons of various shapes and sizes darted back and forth like silver spheres bouncing around inside a pinball game.

"You are Ratsbane."

The smooth voice surprised him; Ratsbane had been so mesmerized by the demonic activity in the room that he had not heard anyone approach him. He turned and instantly recognized Maury, a clever demon inhabiting the body of a green turtle. Large round glasses perched precariously on Maury's nose.

"Yes," Ratsbane answered. "I have been assigned as your new assistant." He extended the directive he had been carrying ever since leaving his sludge mound.

Maury waved at the directive with an air of unconcern. "One more assistant will not matter. I have thirty-seven others to keep track of."

Thirty-seven assistants? Ratsbane's mandibles slackened in disbelief. He knew of no foreman or overdemon with two assistants, and this little green turtle had thirty-seven? *Even when I was in charge of the important PowerLink Prevention Projects,* he remembered, *I only had one assistant at a time—not to mention that they were all incompetent, as well!*

Ratsbane's eyes glowed green with jealousy as Maury escorted him on a tour of RAID. The activity of the demons on the floor reminded Ratsbane of the PIT caverns he had worked in before; he saw nothing new or exceptional here—demons were observing human activity on the monitors and transmitting demonic suggestions via radio waves that could often be picked up by dust particles or mold spores and received by the human ear as thoughts, ideas, or vague impressions.

"I must admit that I'm disappointed," Ratsbane squeaked in his most contemptuous tone. "RAID appears to be nothing more than a well-manned PIT apparatus."

Maury peeked over his glasses at Ratsbane. "Hardware is nothing; strategy is everything," he said.

"What *is* your strategy, then?"

Maury beckoned Ratsbane to follow him. He lumbered slowly to a locked door, pronounced his name aloud, and stood back for Ratsbane as the door swung open.

"How'd you do that?" Ratsbane asked, pointing to the door.

"Oh, that's nothing. We have connections with a top-notch technology firm on the surface," he answered. "Close and lock," he ordered, and the door swung shut behind them in obedient response to Maury's voice command. "Since we demons can create nothing, we must steal what we can, much like Lord Satan does with these bodies we must use."

Ratsbane and Maury stood in the middle of a fully equipped laboratory, with several long tables lined with beakers, burners, and bottles, and other tables and stations furnished with keyboards, screens, modems, and machines.

"This is where the most important work of RAID takes place," Maury said. "For centuries we have been free to try anything—anything—in an effort to keep humans from escaping our clutches and making the PowerLink, the connection between them and the Enemy that breathes life and power and effectiveness into their pitiful souls. We also have unlimited freedom to develop new techniques to disrupt the PowerLink once it has occurred. In recent years," he said, proudly stretching his scrawny turtle neck out from his shell, "we have nearly perfected Project Apple."

"Project Apple?" Ratsbane echoed.

Maury closed his beady little turtle eyes slowly and sighed. "You have not heard of Project Apple?" He opened his eyes and gazed menacingly at Ratsbane.

Ratsbane shrugged. Maury inhaled deeply and continued. "Project Apple is the name of my strategy, a strategy that actually doubles the likelihood that those wretched humans—especially teenagers—will get plastered on a Friday night, or slobber pathetically over some porno flick, or try to punch somebody's lights out."

Maury's breathing quickened, and he reminded Ratsbane of a shark that smells blood.

"My Project Apple—and never forget, Ratsbane, that it's *my* genius that created it—makes kids twice as likely to swipe money from Dad's wallet, three times more likely to mess with drugs, and six times more likely to try to blow their slimy little brains out!

"Thanks to me, we have the technology to double the likelihood that a kid will be disappointed, or resentful, or angry with life!"

"So what's the strategy?" Ratsbane asked.

"Not so fast, mister," Maury answered slyly. "It's taken centuries to reach our current level of effectiveness; I'm not going to jeopardize all that. You can't just come waltzing in here and expect me to spell out my award-winning strategy, just like that." He snapped his fingers to make his point. "I don't even know you yet. How do I know you're not a spy? How do I know I can trust you?"

"I'm a demon, you turtle-faced nerd! Of course, you can't trust me! But you have to tell me what I need to know to do my job."

"Sticks and stones, mister," Maury answered. "Name-calling will get you nowhere. You'll learn the strategy soon enough. Until then, you need to learn your way around RAID."

The Inside Story: News You Can Use

Everybody wants to get the inside story. They want insider information about what stocks to buy. They want the inside scoop on the latest celebrity murder. They want an inside track on a good job opportunity.

The book you're reading is designed to offer you that kind of inside information. It's not an ordinary novel; it's a NovelPlus, a concept created specifically for *The PowerLink Chronicles*. The NovelPlus format allows you to get important information and critical insight in a section called The Inside Story—because this book is not just about Brittney Marsh, Jason Withers, Philip Milford, and the others in the Westcastle Community Church youth group; it's about you. The Inside Story will explain some of the things that are going on in the novel, but it will also help you understand similar things that occur in your life and apply that understanding to yourself.

If you read the first two books in *The PowerLink Chronicles*—*Under Siege* and *The Love Killer*—you already know many of the Westcastle youth group.

You'll get to know them even better in these pages, and you'll come to know a few others, too, such as Bryan Rhoads and Darcelle Davis. You'll also come to know the residents of the demon underworld who are advancing a plot that is intended not only to rob the joy and effectiveness of the Westcastle youth, but eventually to destroy them. Most importantly, it is not only the youth in our story who are the intended victims of that evil plot—the forces of darkness are actually trying to use it on *you* as well (see Eph. 6:10-20)! In the chapters to come, you will discover Satan's main strategy to wear you down, keep you stressed out, make you angry with life, and rob you of satisfaction and fulfillment.

That's the bad news. The *good news* is that you'll also learn how to resist and counter hell's diabolical plot.

2

High in the Sky

Brittney sat in the window seat of the big jetliner, watching the ground crew prepare the plane to leave the gate. A large group from Westcastle Community Church had come to the airport to see her and the other four youth group members off on their six-week trip to Israel. She shook her head, recalling Jason's corny comment to Krystal Wayne after they had prayed together and started for the metal detectors. "I think I'm going to *dig* this place," he said. Krystal had given him a deserved slap on the side of his bald head.

Brittney looked up. People were still boarding the plane. The aisle seat beside her, to which Philip Milford held the ticket, was empty. Philip and Bryan Rhodes blocked the aisle. Bryan was a handsome junior who had moved to Westcastle in the middle of the school year. He had immediately become involved in the youth group and was very vocal at church and at school about his Christian convictions.

"Look," Bryan said to Philip. "It's going to be a long flight—fourteen hours—right?" Philip's expression revealed no interest in Bryan's proposal. "I've got fresh batteries in my GameBoy, and half a dozen games. It's yours for the whole flight, just for trading seats with me."

"Forget it," Philip said. He turned his back on Bryan and flopped into the seat beside Brittney.

Bryan's eyes blazed, and he leaned over Philip to say something further, but saw that Brittney was watching him.

15

He smiled at her and faced the seats across the aisle. Darcelle Davis, an African-American with a wide smile and quiet confidence, sat in the aisle seat. Darcelle had been the one to propose the youth group's participation in an archeological dig in Israel; she had learned of the opportunity through a professor at State College, where she had already enrolled for the fall semester. She had done most of the planning for the trip, and unassumingly functioned as the leader of the group.

Jason sat beside her, an empty seat separating him from a middle-aged woman reading *The Wall Street Journal*. Bryan squeezed past Darcelle and Jason and slumped into the center seat in the section.

The plane rumbled away from the ramp and taxied to the runway. About twenty minutes after the group had all fastened their seat belts and listened to the flight attendant's safety instructions, they felt the craft lift off the ground and point its nose to the sky. They settled in for the fourteen-hour flight to Israel.

Darcelle leaned back in her seat and closed her eyes, while Jason and Bryan bent over a video game. Jason soon tired of Quark, the repetitive video puzzle of interlocking shapes that held Bryan spellbound for long periods, and pulled a magazine out of the pocket in front of him. He leafed through the pages, but his mind soon drifted to the farewell scene at the airport. Pastor and Mrs. Milford had been there, along with Duane and Liz, the leaders of the church's vibrant youth group, and Will McConnell, Amber Lockwood, Krystal Wayne—all members of the youth group. Brittney's mom and Darcelle's mom were there, too, and Bryan's parents found the group just as they were saying good-bye and boarding the plane. Jason had said good-bye to his parents when they left for work early that morning. Jason shook his head slightly and returned the magazine to the seat pocket. He reminded himself that Mom and Dad were good parents. They were just busy; they both had really important jobs, jobs that kept them away from home a lot. The important thing, he told himself, was that they loved him, even though they didn't express it to him very often.

He sighed heavily and glanced across the aisle at Brittney. Her face was turned away from him as she stared out the window.

Brittney watched the clouds roll by beneath the plane. She had made several attempts to start a conversation with Philip, who had made it clear he wasn't thrilled to be on the trip. She eventually decided to leave him alone.

Brittney had known Philip for years through church and school. He was a year ahead of her in school, but they had often been in the same Sunday school class and had occasionally had study halls together. Their relationship had always been friendly, but never close, and lately Philip had begun to change; Brittney knew he was getting into some stuff his parents would not approve of.

Neither of them had become involved in Westcastle Community Church's youth group until recently. Philip had begun attending meetings as a concession to his father, the pastor, and in response to Jason's incessant encouragement; Brittney had joined the youth group not long ago, realizing her need for support from other Christian kids as she began to feel increasingly uncomfortable about her relationship with Matt.

The plane entered a cloud bank and white haze covered Brittney's window like a cottony blanket, reflecting her own confused state of mind. She had begun, long before the plane had left the ground, to dread her six-week absence from Westcastle. She wondered where Matt was, what he was doing, and she began to ache for him with an almost physical pain. He'd tried to call several times since she stood him up at the mall, but she had asked her mother to take a message. He'd even written her a letter; she had thought about throwing it away, but had ended up slipping it, unopened, into her suitcase.

The plane had been in the air about an hour when the attendants began inching down the aisles with a cart filled with drinks. Philip glanced at Brittney; she thought he was about to speak, but he turned to look back up the aisle without saying a word.

"Would you like something to drink, sir?" the blonde attendant asked Philip.

"What do you have?" he asked, inspecting the tray filled with cans and bottles.

The attendant began naming the various beverages available. Philip stopped her.

"I'll just have a Coke," he said.

The woman filled a small plastic cup with Coke and set it down in front of him, then asked the same question of Brittney, who also ordered a Coke. She then turned her attention to Darcelle and the others on the opposite side of the aisle.

As she did so, Philip stole a glance at Brittney; she was staring out the window. He stealthily reached a hand into the flight attendant's cart, extracted two tiny bottles, and stuffed them into the seat pocket in front of him.

Brittney spotted Philip's furtive movements out of the corner of her eye as she turned away from the window. "What are you doing?" Brittney asked. She had clearly seen him hastily stuff two tiny bottles into the pocket of the seat.

"Nothing," he answered. He didn't look at her.

"You can't do that."

"I just did it." He turned and glared at her. The attendant had moved the cart, and Brittney peered around Philip toward Darcelle and Jason. They were paying no attention to Philip and Brittney.

"You'll get us in trouble, Philip."

"No, I won't. Nobody knows—except you and me. And I'm not telling. Are you?"

She shook her head in disapproval. "It's wrong."

He clucked his tongue. "No, it's not."

"It is too. It's stealing." She dropped her voice to a whisper. "Plus, it's alcohol. You're not allowed to have that."

"Lighten up! I get enough preaching at home," he countered. "And anyway, the airline's not going to miss those; they've got plenty."

Brittney looked at him wordlessly.

Philip shrugged. "Look—it may be a big deal to you, but it's not for me, OK? You make it sound like I committed a crime or something."

Brittney tucked her thick brown hair behind her ears. "Philip," she said, her voice betraying her exasperation. "You just better not get us in trouble."

"If you don't say anything, there'll be no trouble—OK?"

Philip crossed his legs beneath his food tray, nearly spilling his drink. He lifted the cup to his mouth and drank its contents quickly.

Philip was still stewing over being forced to go on the youth group trip to Israel. His father had made several conciliatory gestures to Philip, but had refused to change his decision. Not that Philip really expected him to; his father was a hard-nose, in Philip's assessment. He was always telling Philip what to do, and how he should act; he made it clear that he didn't approve of Philip's choice of friends, his choice of music, his choice of anything.

Even when Philip excitedly announced that he'd lined up a sweet summer job at Z103, a local radio station, all his father could say was, "That's the hard rock station." It wasn't a question—it was just a flat statement that effectively communicated his disapproval. That was it. He didn't congratulate Philip, or ask him what his duties would be, or anything like that.

That's the way it was with his father, always. He saw everything in black and white, in rules and restrictions. And his rules drove Philip crazy. *In fact,* Philip thought, *if it wasn't for losing out on that job at the radio station, I might be glad for the chance to get away from home for six weeks. The farther away, the better.*

Philip's thoughts were suddenly interrupted by a commotion behind him. He spun in his seat and looked down the
aisle. The back of the plane was filled with black-coated
Hasidim—orthodox Jews. They were chanting prayers in
Hebrew from tiny black books, rocking back and forth, the
coils of hair that hung from beneath their hats swaying in
rhythm to the fervency of their prayers.

In their midst stood Bryan Rhodes, trying to speak
above the sounds of their praying, waving a shiny tract in his
hand. A slender blonde attendant was speaking to Bryan in
a pleading whisper. The scene became noisier, as Bryan tried
to ignore the prayers of the Jews and the pleading of the attendant, until finally Darcelle leaped from her seat and hur-
ried down the aisle. Philip couldn't make out what anyone
was saying until Darcelle had shepherded Bryan away from
the clot of Jews and back up the aisle.

"They need Jesus just like the rest of us do, Darcelle,"
Bryan said.

"But how would you like it if somebody interrupted
your prayers?" she countered.

"Those aren't prayers," Bryan said earnestly, still facing
the back of the plane as he scooted past a wide-eyed Jason.
"Those are just vain repetitions, like Jesus warned against."

Darcelle just sighed and sank into her seat while Bryan
finally lowered his voice and continued to talk, to Jason.

Philip twisted in his seat again and stared at the group
of black-coated, black-hatted men at the rear of the plane.
Their style of worship was foreign to Philip, but he found
their passion fascinating; they recited their sing-song prayers
with their eyes open, rocking and swaying with their whole
bodies, looking around as they prayed.

He turned to face the front of the plane again, and
glanced at Brittney. Her head lay against the high back of the
seat, and her eyes were closed. Philip wondered what she
was thinking.

☆ ☆ ☆

"Excellent," Maury muttered. "It's going well, don't you think?"

The two demons stood in Maury's laboratory, staring into a high-density video screen. The screen framed the images of Philip and Brittney on the plane. Maury peered at Ratsbane through huge glasses that hugged his nose the way saddlebags hang on a horse. In his scaly hands, he held a thick folder that looked like a school report.

Ratsbane cleared his throat with a rasping squeak. "You mean this Philip guy swiping the liquor?" he asked cautiously.

"Mm hmmm," Maury muttered.

"Well, you're easily amused. When I was a PIT foreman, I had kids having sex, getting pregnant, and getting AIDS. And *that* was before breakfast." His bulbous black eyes glistened with demon delight, just thinking about all the mayhem and human suffering he had been responsible for over the centuries.

"You don't think what just happened is important?"

Ratsbane shrugged. "He sneaked a couple of tiny bottles of booze—big whoopie. I thought your work here was a little bigger than that," he said, an air of sarcasm sneaking into his voice.

Maury whacked Ratsbane on the head with the thick folder in his hands. "You fool!" he cried. "Open your eyes! And your ears! That one little act revealed some important things about that boy and about the girl sitting next to him. Did you hear what he said when the girl told him he was doing something wrong?"

"He said it wasn't."

"Yes, but what did he say next?"

Ratsbane tilted his head. "I don't remember."

"He said, 'It may be a big deal to you, but it's not to me.' And the girl—she stopped arguing right there. That shut her up. Do you see what that tells us?"

"Uh, yeah," Ratsbane answered. "Sure."

Maury slugged him again—hard—with the report. "You lying devil! Those two humans are playing right into my hands." He waved the folder in front of Ratsbane's ant-face. "See this? This is a special report that HAVOC—you know who HAVOC is, don't you?—"

"Yeah, sure," Ratsbane nodded. "Of course, I do."

"How can a demon of hell be such a bad liar?" Maury wondered out loud. "HAVOC is hell's ultra-secret spy service. They obtained this report from one of the Enemy's organizations, and it confirms everything I've been working on! It reveals that concentrating our efforts in one area—*one* area—will practically ensure victory in every other area. By focusing on that *one* area, we can substantially increase our effectiveness in every other area—drug use, pregnancy, violence, stealing, lying, you name it."

Maury waved the HAVOC folder around in the air between them. "Do you know what that one area is, Ratsbane?"

"Uh, yeah, well . . . sure," he stammered, his voice squeaking more than usual. "Yeah. Well, actually, no, I guess."

"It's about truth, Ratsbane! It's all about killing the truth. By making it relative!"

"Relative?" Ratsbane squeaked.

"That's what Project Apple is all about, toadbreath. Philip was telling Brittney that what was wrong for her wasn't necessarily wrong for him. I got him to justify his action so that he didn't think stealing was a big deal in that situation. He believes that truth is relative—get it?"

"Uh, yeah. Yeah, I get it. I guess."

"You don't get it at all, do you?" Maury whacked the side of Ratsbane's head with the file folder. "That's what this report is all about. I've got the research right here." He tapped the folder with a scaly turtle finger. "This confirms even more convincingly than I had been able to prove before.

It's like what the Pestilence Sector has done with AIDS, Ratsbane. They spent thousands of years afflicting humans with colds or flus or pneumonia or melanoma—that was fun, of course, but it had limited success. But once they came up with the AIDS virus, they discovered one affliction that broke down the immune system, making all those diseases deadly effective.

"That's what I've done, Ratsbane! That's the genius of my Project Apple! I've found something that breaks down the moral immune system! I have discovered the moral equivalent of AIDS! I've found a way to get humans to excuse their wrong behavior so that it kills the truth within each individual . . . do you see, Ratsbane?" he asked with a twisted grin. "We've become the Truth Slayers! Ha! Ha-ha-ha! Ha-ha-ha-ha!" Maury laughed maniacally, waving the HAVOC report like a flag, then skipping away like a second-grader on the last day of school.

Ratsbane watched the demon genius leave the well-equipped laboratory that produced his diabolical plan. He waited for the laboratory door to close.

"Truth slayers?" he muttered. He shook his head. "I'm working for the biggest idiot in hell!"

The Inside Story:
The Club

Imagine being approached by a friend at school.

"Hey," your friend says, "have you heard about the club?"

"You mean that thing people put on their steering wheels so no one can steal their car?"

"No, I mean the new club—the new organization everyone's talking about."

"I haven't heard a thing," you answer.

"Where have you been? It's the best! Look, I got a membership card all filled out for you."

"Wait a minute," you say. "What do I get for joining?"

"Well, for one, just by joining you can double your tendency to get drunk or steal, and triple your chances of getting involved in illegal drug use!"

"Why would I want to do that?" you say, but your friend seems not to hear.

"You'll become two times more likely to feel disappointed and resentful, two times more likely to lack purpose, and six times more likely to attempt suicide!"

Would you join a club like that? No? Well, believe it or not, you may already be a member.

Philip's petty theft on the plane, for example, may not seem terribly important. After all, swiping a little bottle of liquor isn't like murdering someone. And everybody does something wrong now and then.

But it's wasn't the liquor—nor even the fact that Philip stole it—that excited the demon, Maury. He was elated, not by the act itself, but by what it—and Philip's conversation with Brittney—revealed about the success of his plan among the Westcastle youth.

When Philip said to Brittney, "It may be a big deal to you, but it's not for me," he was expressing, in his own way, his lack of a belief in absolute truth. His statement reflected a "relativistic view," a rationalization that justified his behavior. Wrong became acceptable to Philip. And Brittney, though she sensed that what he did was wrong, wasn't all too sure about it herself.

As Maury explained to Ratsbane, the key to the success of Project Apple was making truth relative or situational, not absolute, in the minds of people.

You see, some people believe that truth is absolute; that is, they believe that there are some things that are true **for all people, for all times, and for all places.** Others, of course, don't accept an absolute standard of truth; they believe extenuating circumstances can change a wrong for one person into a right for another. When a person accepts that view, they are saying the individual has the right to legitimize certain things that at one time everyone accepted as wrong. This way of thinking says that there is no absolute right and wrong that governs a person's life and, in a way, the truth and its benefits are slain.

Maury knows that students who don't believe that absolute truth really exists (or that it can be known with any degree of certainty) are far more likely to engage in inappropriate behavior than young people who believe in an absolute standard of right and wrong because they will feel free to justify their behavior. Not only that—he knows that the lack of a firm belief in truth makes students more likely to be unhappy and dissatisfied with their lives. In other words, if you don't believe in absolute standards of truth and morality, you're already a member of that club we discussed a few pages ago.

The report that Maury obtained from HAVOC (hell's counter-intelligence agency) was a survey of 3,795 church kids commissioned by Josh McDowell Ministry. The research, conducted among youth of thirteen different denominations by The Barna Research Group, revealed that what a teenager believes about truth affects his or her behavior *and* happiness.

For example, kids who don't accept an objective standard of truth are:

- 36 percent more likely to lie to a parent or other adult
- 48 percent more likely to cheat on an exam
- 2 times more likely to try to physically hurt someone
- 2 times more likely to watch a pornographic film
- 2 times more likely to get drunk
- 2 1/2 times more likely to steal

- 3 times more likely to use illegal drugs
- 6 times more likely to attempt suicide

People's views about right and wrong not only affect their behavior, however; they also affect their attitudes. For example, teens who do not embrace truth as an objective standard that governs their lives are:

- 65 percent more likely to mistrust people
- 2 times more likely to be disappointed
- 2 times more likely to be angry with life
- 2 times more likely to lack purpose
- 2 times more likely to be resentful

You see, when you believe in an absolute standard for distinguishing right from wrong—that certain things are right **for all people, for all times, for all places**—you acknowledge that there are fundamental moral and ethical guidelines that exist independently of your personal opinion. You acknowledge that the distinction between right and wrong is:

- objective (it is defined outside yourself—an attitude or action cannot be justified subjectively within yourself),
- universal (it is **for all people in all places**—extenuating circumstances cannot change it from person to person or place to place), and
- constant (it is for all times—it cannot be successfully argued that it does not apply to your generation).

When you accept an objective standard for truth, you adopt a moral and ethical viewpoint that guides your choices of what is right and what is wrong. Your "truth view" acts as a lens through which you see all of life and its many choices.

When you view life through the lens of truth, you are better able to discern the "real" truth and distinguish what is really right from what is really wrong; you will be better equipped to identify what truths are absolute and what makes them absolute . . . and you'll have a fighting chance to make the right choices.

That's why truth is the key to hell's strategy. Because what you believe about truth will affect the choices you make—choices between right and wrong, and between fulfillment and frustration.

3

A Man Named Shebtai

Darcelle shook Jason awake.

"We're landing, Jason," she said. Jason lifted his head and blinked. Darcelle continued, "I don't see how you can sleep like that. I haven't slept at all." They had been in the air for more than twelve hours; the flight attendant had announced that they would be landing at approximately 11:00 A.M. local time.

She reached across the aisle. Philip sprawled in his seat, his legs flung into the aisle and his head slumped against Brittney's shoulder. Darcelle tapped Philip's knee. He groaned without opening his eyes, but Brittney, who had been watching the plane's descent out the window, signaled that she would help rouse Philip.

After coaxing her seatmate's eyes open, Brittney returned her gaze to the view outside her window. A thin stretch of beach separated the sparkling blue-green waters of the Mediterranean from the modern city of Tel Aviv. Brittney blinked in surprise at the sprawling city beneath the plane, the economic and social center of the nation of Israel. As the plane descended toward the airport east of the city, she was able to make out more details, noting especially the many adobe-type dwellings with dull white domes sprinkled among the roofs.

She lifted her gaze and saw green slopes giving way to brown peaks in the distance and, as the plane circled, a seemingly endless plain to the south. She was seeing Israel for the first time—the land of Jesus, the land of Abraham, Isaac, and Jacob—and it seemed strange to her to be arriving in an airplane.

Across the aisle, Jason turned to Darcelle.

"Is my hair messed up?" Jason's face wore a look of feigned concern. Darcelle glanced briefly at Jason's bald head. "Made you look," he said quickly, pointing a finger at Darcelle and smiling victoriously.

Darcelle rolled her eyes, but smiled back. She nodded at the empty seat beyond Jason. "Where's Bryan?"

He shrugged. "Probably being a pain somewhere else, which is fine with me."

"Jason!" she admonished.

"We're not even in Israel yet and he's already offended or embarrassed nearly everyone on the plane."

"He means well, Jason," she said ruefully.

"Can we buy him a shirt that says, *I'm not with them*?"

Darcelle prepared to respond, but Bryan appeared and squeezed by several people and into his seat beside Jason.

Thirty minutes later the giant plane rumbled up to Gate 47 at Ben Gurion airport east of Tel Aviv. As the group from Westcastle claimed their baggage, Bryan Rhodes appeared at Brittney's side. He wrestled her bags off the conveyor belt and stuffed them under his arms as he lifted his own bags by the handles.

"I can carry my own bags, Bryan," she argued. He looked ridiculous, and she felt silly letting him carry so much luggage while she chased after him empty-handed. He insisted that his load was *not heavy*, and *his burden was light*. Brittney rolled her eyes and entered the line of travelers inching their way through customs together.

High fence-like dividers enclosed the area, and uniformed men and women stood around holding rifles. Dingy signs bearing messages in German, Hebrew, English, and French were posted at various points throughout the dimly lit area. A babel of unrecognizable languages surrounded Darcelle and the others, and many unfamiliar smells—of foods and fabrics, oils and human perspiration—seemed to exude from the bodies and clothes of their fellow travelers.

Brittney was the last to show her passport to the official, while Bryan and Jason waited for her; like the others, she answered a series of questions and was waved through the checkpoint. They joined Philip and Darcelle and walked in a clumsy caravan through the bustling airport.

"Darcelle," Jason whispered as they approached the doors leading to the street. He jerked his head in the direction of the exit. "Some guy's got a piece of cardboard with your name on it over there."

"Where?" she asked.

Jason turned and, without setting either of his suitcases down, waved his head in the direction of a middle-aged man dressed in khaki pants and a blue-and-white striped shirt. A gray beard framed his face, and his forehead extended high into a head of unruly gray hair. Darcelle thanked Jason and approached the man.

"I'm Darcelle Davis," she said. Bryan, Brittney, Jason, and Philip stood in a neat half-circle behind her.

"Welcome to Eretz Israel," the man answered. A smile spread across a deeply tanned face. "My name is Shebtai Levitt. I am your host." He reached out and gripped both of Darcelle's suitcases; he shoved one into Philip's hand and the other under one of Jason's arms. Then he turned and walked briskly through the glass doors leading out of the airport.

Jason and Philip helped Shebtai load the luggage into the back of a dust-covered Land Rover, a box-like vehicle that looked like a cross between an army Jeep and a Chevy Blazer. Darcelle sat in the front seat, while the others squeezed into the seat in the back; Bryan cunningly offered his lap to Brittney, but she squeezed her thin form between Jason and the side of the vehicle.

The noisy Land Rover rattled and bounced into traffic as Shebtai Levitt steered out of the airport and onto Highway 40, a two-lane highway that resembled the county roads around Westcastle. The windows in the Land Rover were down and Levitt spoke loudly, asking questions through the noise, heat, and dust of the traffic.

As he drove, he pointed to features in the Judean countryside, relating each to a facet of Israel's history. He pointed to the barren, rocky slopes and peaks of the Yehuda, or Judah, Mountains to the east, detailing stories of David, who hid himself and his armies from King Saul in those mountains.

He swept his hand across the dirty windshield in front of Darcelle and pointed across the flat coastal plain toward the cities of Ashdod and Ashkelon, ancient cities of the Philistines, which housed the Ark of God in the time of Samuel. He related how, when the ark was placed in the temple of the Philistine god Dagon, the statue of Dagon repeatedly toppled to its face before the ark of the God of Israel. When the people of Ashdod were afflicted with tumors, they sent the ark to Gath, where the same thing happened. The people of Gath sent the ark to Ekron until the Philistines finally got smart and shipped the ark of the covenant back to Israel.

Shebtai's eyes sparkled as he related the fascinating stories of Israel's history. He told the stories with an intensity that captivated his listeners and made them forget the thoughts that had occupied them on the plane.

For the next four hours, Shebtai related tales of ancient and modern Israel as they passed through the cities of Kiryat Gat and Beer Sheva, and into the brown and arid Negev, the narrow wedge of land that separates Egypt from Jordan. At one point, Shebtai pulled the Land Rover to the side of the road and turned off the engine. Without a word to any of them, he walked alone into the sand and rocks of the countryside. Philip, Bryan, Brittney, Jason, and Darcelle exchanged quizzical looks as they watched him from the Land

Rover. He stopped after walking for five minutes or more; it looked like he was rocking back and forth like the Hasidic Jews on the plane, though at that distance none of them could be sure what he was doing.

He returned without hurrying, and climbed into the vehicle. He offered no explanation for his strange behavior, and they continued their hot, dry drive on the two-lane road until they arrived at the town of Mizpeh Ramon. There Shebtai stopped to fill the Land Rover's gas tank and buy a small bag of items at a tiny Arab grocery. He then drove yet further into the stony countryside.

At last, Shebtai turned off the road and steered the Land Rover onto a rocky path that tossed and shook the travelers like human pinballs.

"Ow!" Bryan cried. "Take it easy!"

"I am very sorry," Shebtai shouted over the whine of the engine and the sound of crunching rocks beneath the tires. "When I first came to Har Karkom several years ago, the only way to reach the site was on pack animals. This jeep trail makes things much easier."

Brittney, Jason, Bryan, and Philip held on to the Land Rover's jiggling roof, walls, and to each other as the vehicle rocked and tipped along the uneven path.

"The Desert of Paran," Shebtai said, with a sweeping gesture to indicate the sun-baked plain to the south, "is where the Israelites wandered for thirty-eight years before entering the land God had promised them." His tanned, bearded face wore a look of pride, as though he were showing off a personal accomplishment.

The group finally arrived at an assortment of Jeeps and tents, and Shebtai maneuvered the Land Rover into a narrow space between a tent and a large gray tank. He showed them to the tents that would be their homes for the next six weeks. Each tent, furnished with three cots, allowed just enough room for their luggage. Brittney and Darcelle shared a tent, as did the three boys. Shebtai informed them that the other tents housed volunteers from all over the world: Ethiopian Jews, Italian college students, and a few Israelis like himself. He informed them that they would be allowed a brief period to get settled in, and then he would escort them to the mess tent for an orientation meeting.

Shebtai waved his hand to the group and opened the screen door of a large tent.

Brittney, Jason, Philip, Bryan, and Darcelle stepped inside and looked around. Six or seven rickety tables filled the tent.

Shebtai instructed everyone to be seated so he could explain the rules, procedures, and schedule of the dig. "I have been dig director at Har Karkom for almost two decades, and I have worked with many volunteers in that time," Shebtai explained in his curt Israeli accent. "The rules we follow here are the result of experience, and everything is set up the way it is because it works, hm?" He raised his salt-and-pepper eyebrows and cast a questioning glance at the group.

Philip frowned and leaned his lips close to Brittney's ear. "Hard-nose," he whispered.

Jason glanced quickly at Brittney; she met his eyes and he looked quickly back at Shebtai.

"The rules are few, but they are important," Shebtai continued. "One, males and females must not enter each other's tents . . . at any time. Two, the day begins at four o'clock every morning, so a nine o'clock curfew will be enforced."

"Nine o'clock?" Philip blurted. "You've got to be joking!"

"After a few days of work," Shebtai said, "you will be very happy when nine o'clock arrives."

Brittney looked with interest from Philip to Shebtai.

"Three, removing any tool or artifact from the site," Shebtai continued, as if he had repeated the words many times before, "no matter how small, is not permitted. Four, shoes and shirts must be worn at all times. Five, breakfast will be eaten on site, lunch and dinner will be available at one o'clock and six o'clock; if you come late you will go hungry. These are the commandments of Shebtai Levitt, your dig director," he intoned with a smile. "Happy are you if you keep them."

"What happens if you break a rule?" Philip asked.

"You get a demerit," Shebtai answered matter-of-factly. "Three demerits . . . you go home." Shebtai's pronouncement was met with a moment of shocked silence.

Philip hung his head. "I thought I left my father at home."

Shebtai went on to explain the schedule: every Thursday was laundry and shopping day in Mizpeh Ramon. He would take all newcomers on a complete walking tour of the mountain next Sunday, and later in the six-week term, he would plan sightseeing trips to Jerusalem, Bethlehem, and Masada and the Dead Sea.

A red-haired girl with dark eyes suddenly emerged from the kitchen. Jason, Philip, and Bryan immediately straightened themselves to their full height, and self-consciously combed their hair with their fingers or wiped their hands on their pants.

Shebtai introduced the sixteen-year-old Israeli beauty as Avi, short for Avitar. He explained that she worked in the kitchen, and falteringly introduced each member of the group to her. She smiled broadly, nodded at each of the newcomers, and walked back in the direction of the kitchen. The boys in the group watched her departure with interest.

He next led the group on a tour of the dig, showing them the various sites where work was being done. He pointed out the prolific rock art that characterized Har Karkom. He pointed to one rock that bore an image that looked like a human eye with many rays emanating outward.

"It's called an eye of God," he explained. Like much of the rock art on and around Har Karkom, it had spiritual significance to ancient people. Shebtai seemed to attach special meaning to a large flint rock that displayed a twisting snake next to a staff, and another rock that bore the image of a grid divided into ten spaces in a hopscotch design.

He showed them the various sites where they would be working; their jobs, for the first few days at least, would consist primarily of shoveling dirt and debris into buckets, hauling it to a designated spot, and dumping it. The tour ended at the summit of Har Karkom, the place is called Mount Saffron in English.

"It is a special place," Shebtai said, as they stood 2,795 feet above sea level and gazed across the southern Negev. The half-mile climb from camp had been taxing, but Shebtai seemed less winded than the teenagers. The group looked out from the eastern side of the mountain to the arid vista below. Bryan shouldered himself between Brittney and Jason, and gripped her hand.

"It's beautiful, isn't it?" he said, fastening his eyes on hers.

Brittney's lip curled with confusion. She didn't think it was beautiful at all. And Bryan's attempts at charm made her long for Matt, made her wish she had not come on this trip. She pried her hand out of Bryan's grip and flashed him an annoyed look.

"It is harsh, and it is desolate," Shebtai was saying as he looked down from the loaf-shaped mountain to the wide plain below, "but it is a special place. You are very lucky to be here."

4

Broken Rules and Broken Hearts

The next day began at 4:00 A.M.

Darcelle and Brittney were already in the camp kitchen, standing around the table, making sack breakfasts and chatting with Avi. The young Israeli had spent only a few hours with them during free time last evening, but the group—especially Bryan and Philip—had already come to accept her.

Jason stumbled in the door of the mess tent as they spoke.

"I can't believe this," he muttered sourly. He came to a stop across the table from the three girls. "What are we going to do, dig by candlelight?"

Darcelle slapped a spoonful of jam on half of a bread roll and extended it across the table in the palm of her hand. "Are Bryan and Philip up?" she asked.

"Yeah." Jason devoured the bread and jam in two bites. "They're not quite as cheerful in the morning as I am."

"Oh, yeah," Brittney offered. "You're a barrel of laughs."

She smiled prettily at him, and he immediately wished he had given a better impression.

Bryan entered in time to witness Brittney and Jason's playful exchange. He answered the others' cheerful greetings with a serious nod, circled the table, and squeezed between Brittney and Avi.

"What's for breakfast?" he asked, addressing himself only to the girls on both sides of him. "What you see is what you get," Brittney answered, indicating the food on the table and nonchalantly stepping away from Bryan.

"Avi will help you get your breakfast together," Darcelle explained to Bryan. She and Avi exchanged smiles. "We leave for the site at 5:00 A.M., work for about three hours, and then take a break for breakfast. Then we work until 12:30 or 1:00 P.M. and return to camp for the rest of the day."

Jason watched the scene with dismay. Bryan never seemed uncomfortable around girls; he acted like he fully expected girls to like him, and usually they did. But it just wasn't that easy for Jason. If he wasn't joking around, he never knew what to say. He was always afraid of doing or saying the wrong thing, always afraid to open up, always afraid of being rejected.

Philip strode through the door, and approached them with a smile. "Hi, Avi," he said. The redheaded beauty smiled.

Darcelle and Brittney exchanged glances.

"What about us?" Brittney asked. He answered her protest with a good-natured smile. "You're in a much better mood than you were yesterday," she added.

His eyes flitted toward the redheaded girl. He grinned. "Archaeology is my life," he said. He turned to Avi again, ignoring the others. "Can I help you with anything?"

Shebtai arrived a few moments later and drove the group to the dig. He introduced them to the various staff, people who oversaw specific aspects of the work, such as pottery excavation and dating. He then explained the laborious process of working the dig. He handed pickaxes to Brittney and Darcelle, and buckets to the boys, and demonstrated their jobs.

The sun and dirt, perhaps the two most significant features of the Negev, made for a gritty, grungy morning of work. Brittney and Darcelle shoveled sand and rocks into buckets, which Bryan, Philip, and Jason toted, two at a time, to a distant dumping area. Shebtai, wearing a short-sleeved shirt and long tan pants, appeared and disappeared regularly, instructing, encouraging, occasionally grabbing a tool and working alongside one of the volunteers. He seemed capable of being everywhere at once, of responding to a call for help before it was issued.

The Westcastle youth grunted and groaned under the hard work, and very soon they were rubbing sore hands and stretching sore backs. But everyone was working hard, and even as they tired, they felt themselves becoming stronger; the sweat that trickled down their faces and backs as they worked and the dirt that lodged under their fingernails somehow filled them with a mysterious satisfaction.

The atmosphere of the dig was one of contagious optimism, in which all seemed to feel they were not just digging and hauling dirt, they were uncovering civilizations. Every worker imagined that the next swing of the ax or the next bucket of dirt might uncover a priceless ancient artifact—a precious discovery that would make its discoverer an instantaneous international hero.

Darcelle and Brittney chatted off and on as they loosened dirt and dug trenches with their pickaxes; Bryan, Philip, and Jason traded only occasional comments as they passed each other on their way to and from the dumping area.

On one of his return trips with empty buckets, Jason jogged up to Darcelle and Brittney.

"Hey, guys," he whispered. He tossed his head behind him. "Look over there."

The girls looked in the direction Jason had indicated and saw Shebtai, standing fifteen or twenty feet beyond the excavation area, immobile, staring farther up the mountain.

"What's he looking at?" Brittney asked, her eyes fixed on Shebtai's form.

"I don't know," Jason answered, not looking at Shebtai, but studying Brittney's features. "He's been doing that for the last five minutes."

"Just standing there?" Darcelle asked.

Brittney turned her head and met Jason's glance. He blushed at being caught staring at her. He avoided her eyes and looked back up the slope at Shebtai.

"He's a strange man, isn't he?" she said.

The trio was quiet for a few moments, until Darcelle said, "Yeah. But there's something about him . . . "

"Yeah—something," Brittney said, identifying with Darcelle's admiring tone. "Something that makes you want to be around him, makes you want to know what he's thinking."

They returned, filthy and sweaty, to camp after seven hours of hard work. Avi met them in the mess tent, and they shared a lunch of pita bread stuffed with falafel, cucumbers, and tomatoes.

"I am glad you are here," Avi said, as they ate together. Even when she spoke to the entire group, she always addressed herself to Darcelle or Brittney. She spoke excellent English. "The volunteers are usually college students or older people. It is nice to meet some people my own age. Usually I have just my father to talk to."

"Your father?" Philip asked.

Avi's eyebrows wrinkled over her dark eyes, then lifted again with understanding. "He did not tell you when he introduced me," she said, remembering. "I am Avitar *Levitt*," she said. "Shebtai's daughter."

"You mean that weird old guy is you fa—," Bryan's words stuck in his mouth as he saw the wounded look that immediately crossed Avi's face. He cleared his throat awkwardly and began to say something else when Darcelle spoke.

"Shebtai is your father," she said, smiling.

Avi nodded and returned Darcelle's smile. "I have spent every summer at Har Karkom since I was a baby. My mother died when I was young, so it has been just Father and me since then." She dropped her knife into the dirt and asked Darcelle to reach behind her for a clean knife. Darcelle pulled a knife from a drawer, and Avi quickly corrected her. "Not from *that* drawer," she said, pointing to a seemingly identical set of utensils on the table. "I need one of those knives over there."

Darcelle pulled a table knife from the rack and handed it to Avi. "What's the difference?" she asked.

"We keep a *kosher* kitchen," she answered, which means one set of dishes is used for meals that include meat, and another set for meals that include milk, or cheese, or butter. She began to spread jam onto a scrap of pita bread.

"How do you keep all the rules straight around here?" Philip asked.

Avi shrugged. "It is not hard," she answered. "It is just the way we live."

"Don't you get tired of being here so much?" Philip asked. "I mean, there's nothing to do but eat, sleep, and work."

Avi shook her head. "Like Father says, it is a special place. And there are other things to do." She looked around the mess tent and dropped her voice to a whisper. "There is a water hole big enough for swimming not far from here," she said.

"Yeah!" Philip said, imagining Avi in a swimsuit. "When can we go?"

Avi promised to take them as soon as possible, perhaps later in the week, after the Thursday laundry and shopping trip to Mizpeh Ramon. They gathered up the scraps of their lunch, disposed of them, and began to file out of the mess tent in a tight group. Jason held the door open for Brittney and Darcelle, while Bryan and Philip jostled for position beside Avi.

"Do you go into that town," Bryan asked Avi, referring to Mizpeh Ramon, "whenever your father goes?"

Avi answered without meeting Bryan's gaze. "I like to help Father with the shopping."

Bryan smiled smugly and glanced at Philip briefly before turning his eyes fully on Avi. "I was hoping we could go . . . together, you know—you show me around a little."

Avi stopped walking, and both boys stopped with her. "I was already planning," she said, speaking slowly and turning to smile at Philip, "to go with Philip . . . into town."

Philip's eyes registered surprise.

Avi shrugged and turned a smiling face toward Bryan. "I'm sorry," she said.

Bryan's face blushed but otherwise wore no expression. "No problem," he shrugged, and walked on, leaving them standing outside the mess tent.

"Gosh, I hope you don't mind," she said, "There's just something about that guy."

He swallowed. "No, no, I don't mind." He grinned broadly as his wide eyes gawked at the red-headed beauty.

Brittney and Darcelle fell into bed a few minutes before nine o'clock that evening, feeling the effects of their long journey and a demanding day of labor.

"I told you we wouldn't mind the curfew," Darcelle said. "We've only been here a day, and I'm exhausted." She sprawled on her cot and began reading her Bible by the light of the hissing gas lamp on the wooden box between her cot—farthest from the door—and Brittney's.

Brittney extracted an envelope from her suitcase and unfolded the letter that had been packed inside.

"A letter from your mom?" Darcelle asked, nodding at the sheets of stationery Brittney held in her hands.

Brittney shook her head. "From Matt."

"I thought you two broke up." Darcelle's voice was soft, soothing, a voice that invited trust.

"I broke up with him," Brittney said in a quivering voice, her eyes filling with tears. She wrestled with her emotions for a moment, and finally continued, quietly. "I didn't want . . . to do the same things he wanted to do."

"Good for you, girl," Darcelle said. She closed her Bible and placed it on the box beside the lamp. "I hope you set him straight." She tilted her head to look into Brittney's eyes. "You want to talk about it?"

Brittney shook her head. She didn't want to admit to Darcelle how she felt. She remembered how slowly she had been able to put the guilt to sleep—how thrilling her intimacy with Matt had been, but how awful she had felt afterward, not just the first time but every time, and how the thrill diminished and her guilt and emptiness increased—but she couldn't seem to overcome the pain of her separation from him. She didn't want to tell her friend Darcelle that she'd rather be back in Westcastle right now, with Matt.

The hissing lamp beside her cot gave off such fierce heat that Brittney soon found herself sweating. Darcelle had rolled over after their brief conversation and had fallen asleep quickly. Brittney had read Matt's letter several times, and had felt her eyes well with tears of homesickness and regret, when she heard a noise outside her tent. She sat straight, prepared to wake Darcelle at the first sign of trouble.

Moments passed, and there was no further noise. She stuffed the letter back into her dusty suitcase and stood. The tent seemed unbearably stuffy.

Brittney leaned over the wooden crate and turned the tiny disc on the lamp; the light diminished to a dull glow. She paused to make sure the lamp would not go out completely, then lifted the triangular flap door of the tent and stepped out into the night.

The coolness in the air invigorated her like a cup of cold water poured over a distance runner's head. The camp was quiet, and she stood for a moment outside her tent, getting her bearings and letting her eyes adjust to the starry darkness. She finally determined her location and set out in the direction of the mess tent.

She had walked no more than ten paces when something skittered or slithered across the ground in front of her. She leaped back and coiled her upper body into a tight knot like a snake that had been startled.

I don't know what that was, she said to herself, *and I'd like to keep it that way.*

"Who are you?"

A male voice behind her made her straighten. She swallowed.

"Turn around please," the voice said.

She turned slowly. A man, not much taller than her, stood several feet from her. He pointed a rifle at her.

"Who are you?" he repeated. "What are you doing?"

"I'm Britt—" She coughed nervously. "Brittney Marsh. I'm—I'm one of the volunteers. I'm just taking a walk."

"It's after curfew." He waved his rifle. "I will walk you back to your tent."

Brittney stood, immobile, until he stepped aside and motioned for her to lead the way. She returned to her tent, the man with the rifle following closely behind.

"You should get some sleep." He stood outside her tent. "Morning comes early at Har Karkom."

She ducked into the tent. As the door flapped shut behind her, she stepped to the glowing lamp and turned the little knob until the light died. Then she undressed and lay down on her cot. Darcelle had not stirred.

"That was weird," she whispered out loud. She consulted the glowing dial of her watch and saw that it was well past curfew. "Who does he think he is? I'm almost sixteen; I don't need someone telling me that I can't go for a walk by myself. Anyway, these tents are hot and stuffy, and I don't have to stay locked up in one of them like an animal!"

She swung her bare feet over the edge of the cot, and was about to stand when she remembered the slithery thing that had crossed her path moments ago. She lifted her feet quickly and swept them back onto the bed.

"I just don't feel like it—that's all," she whispered.

☆ ☆ ☆

Ratsbane sat in a semi-circular command center before the high-density video screen in Maury's well-equipped laboratory. His toad-like feet were propped on the desk of the command console, which sparkled and glittered with flashing lights like the bridge of *Star Trek's* USS Enterprise.

He balanced a large keyboard on his lap and leisurely punched commands into the computer. Suddenly, the door swung open and the green turtle form of Maury skipped in. He instructed the electronic door to close and lock itself, and then waddled over to the command center.

Upon Maury's entrance, Ratsbane swept his feet off the console and returned the keyboard to the counter.

"What's the status of those kids?" Maury asked.

Ratsbane scrambled for the keyboard and punched a few buttons; the images on the screen began to move quickly in reverse. He and Maury watched it in silence for a few moments until Ratsbane pressed two keys simultaneously and the images returned to normal.

"Here," Ratsbane said, pointing to the screen. "I pulled this off just a few minutes ago."

He replayed the incident outside Brittney's tent. Maury watched with interest.

"So she went for a walk," Maury said. "And got caught breaking curfew. So?"

Ratsbane turned his ant-head and peered through marble-black eyes at Maury. "What do you mean, *So?*"

Maury looked at his fellow demon peevishly and made an airy sound with his turtle beak. "I hope that's not the best you've got."

"What do you mean? Don't you see? I got her doing the same kinds of things that the boy was doing on the plane. Now *she's* doing something wrong."

"Don't focus on her *doing* wrong, toad-face—focus on her defending her actions by convincing herself that the wrong thing was actually right for her. You need to use the little stuff, like the discomfort of a stuffy tent, to get her to justify breaking the rules." Maury shoved Ratsbane aside and began pushing buttons on the keyboard.

"Now listen carefully to the girl's thoughts," he said. A string of moving letters scrolled across the large screen. "I don't need someone telling me that I can't go for a walk by myself. Anyway, these tents are hot and stuffy and I don't have to stay locked up in one of them like an animal!"

"With that kind of attitude," Maury said, "we can move in for the kill." He turned a glaring eye toward Ratsbane.

"I know that," Ratsbane whined in his own defense.

"Maybe you do, and maybe you don't. Just remember, you odious toad, that you must convince her, little by little, bit by bit, to justify her wrong attitudes, to excuse her wrong behavior, that she and she alone determines what's right for her, and that no-body—*nobody*," he growled, "has the right to impose his views on her. You must convince her that there are no standards, no absolutes, to look to, except those standards she determines within herself."

"I *know* that," Ratsbane repeated.

"Maybe you do, and maybe you don't," Maury spat back venomously.

The Inside Story:
Adam's Family

Brittney's got a problem. She is chafing at the rules someone else has established, rules she views as denying her the right to do what she feels is right for herself.

Her problem is nothing new. As a matter of fact, it's as old as the struggle between devils and humans.

It started with the serpent's strategy in the Garden of Eden. The snake snuck up behind the woman.

"Yo, Mama," he said (even though she wasn't a mother yet). "How come you haven't tried that fruit tree at the center of the garden?"

"God said not to," she answered.

"He really said you couldn't eat from all these fruity trees?" He would have swept an arm around to indicate the many fruit trees that surrounded them, but serpents don't have arms.

"No," she answered. "He just said we couldn't eat from that tree—couldn't even touch it, I think He said, or we would die."

"Aw, you're kidding me! You won't die from touching that ol' tree. God just doesn't want you going near it because He knows if you eat that fruit you'll become like Him."

Now, Eve must have looked very puzzled, hearing a comment like that.

"Hey, let me break it down for you, Mama—let me make it really simple. God is saying He's the only One who can define what is truly right and wrong. And, to make things worse, He's got the gall to try to impose it on you. That's not right, Mama; you deserve to eat from that tree. You have what it takes to determine for yourself whether the fruit is good or evil. Just because He says it's evil doesn't make it evil. You don't have to accept His ideas. You have the right to decide what's good for you and what's bad for you on your own—just like God does. Now, doesn't that sound good?"

The serpent's rap worked, of course, and Eve ate the fruit. The serpent had convinced her that she was perfectly capable of judging between good and evil. He persuaded her to believe that she didn't need God to define right and wrong, but that she could decide such things on her own; that she didn't need an outside, objective standard, but could be her *own* standard. She later convinced her husband, Adam, to eat, got kicked out of the garden, and went on to raise Adam's family.

We are now all part of Adam and Eve's family, and Satan's strategy is the same now as then. He wants to prevent men and women from looking to God as the objective standard, the only true definer of right and wrong, and instead prompt them to look to themselves to justify what they do as right in their own eyes.

For centuries, that plan met with limited success; most men and women still looked to God as the objective righteous Judge. They viewed God as the One who said what was right was right and what was wrong was wrong. In the words of one author, "They were convinced that God's revelation . . . was true. True in an absolute sense. It was not merely true to them; it was not merely true in their time; it was not true approximately. What God had given was true universally, absolutely, and enduringly."[1]

But recent centuries—and particularly the past several decades—have brought about a significant shift in the way many men and women think. Our society has largely rejected the notions of truth and morality; it has lost the ability (or the willingness) to recognize that there is an absolute right (and an absolute wrong) that exists independently of what you or I think or believe.

Many public schools promote value-free, morally neutral education. "We cannot tell you," the teachers and textbooks say, "what is wrong and what is right. You must decide that for yourselves." Politicians, afraid of offending parts of their constituency, avoid taking a stand on moral grounds. The media exalt ideas and behavior that challenge all traditional concepts of morality.

As a result, recent generations have increasingly relied on their own ideas of morality. Like Philip Milford, they become their own gods, establishing their own standards, from within, that determine what is right and wrong for them. And, like Brittney Marsh, they resist suggestions that someone else has determined what's right and what's wrong for them.

In so doing, however, they are like a sailor on the ocean who tries to determine his location by pointing himself in a direction—any direction—and calling it north. He will eventually get lost if he measures his position only by himself (instead of looking to the heavens and charting his course by the north star), because "north" is not an opinion or a preference.

Similarly, if we try to determine the right or wrong of an action by ourselves, we're certain to eventually get lost. We are all members of Adam's family, but we do not need to repeat Adam and Eve's mistake. We can look to heaven, to the Judge of heaven and earth, and learn—and accept—that He and He alone is the standard and definition of good and evil.

5

Mistakes and Misbehavior

Jason, Philip, and Bryan came running at the sound of Darcelle's scream.

She and Brittney, after several days of using a pickax to break up dirt and gather it into buckets, had been assigned to a new area where, on the perimeter of a grid of roped-off dirt squares, they used small brushes and dentists' picks to clear dirt and debris from specimens of rock art.

"We found something," Brittney announced breathlessly. "It's a drawing."

Shebtai appeared immediately; he stood over the dug-out area where the girls worked and issued occasional instructions, sometimes kneeling, sometimes pointing, watching every move with an intensity that seemed capable of starting fires, like a ray of sun focused through a magnifying glass.

The boys crowded against a balk, the wall of an excavation square, as Darcelle and Brittney worked together with a small pick and brush to free a dark sandstone rock that contained a reddish carving of a simple stick figure. They worked patiently as the temperature climbed throughout the morning, and by noon had uncovered what appeared to be the entire carving.

Darcelle stood to stretch her back, and climbed out of the trench. Brittney turned to look up at her friend.

"What do you think it is?" Brittney asked, pointing to the stylized characters on the rock.

Darcelle shrugged. "That one," she said, pointing to the stick figure on the left, "looks like a person doing jumping jacks or something." She leaned her head to one side. "The other thing," she said, hesitating, "I don't know. It doesn't look like anything."

"It is most likely," Shebtai interjected, "a picture of a man praying with arms lifted toward the heavens."

Brittney nodded. "Yeah, I can see that."

"It is a common posture for prayer among Jews."

"What about that line beside the man?" Darcelle asked.

"The same image has been found many times here at Har Karkom—a man praying beside a simple vertical line or some other equally—" he hesitated, searching for the word "—abstract figure."

"What does it mean?" Brittney asked.

"It is probably the attempt of an ancient people—that rock carving may be four or five thousand years old—to depict the worship of a God who could not be drawn, who could not be portrayed as a man or an animal . . . or who had forbidden people from doing so."

The group stared at the reddish engraving on the black rock.

"Wow," said Brittney. She looked at Darcelle, who was smiling proudly.

"You think this could have been made by an Israelite?" Jason asked. "And that straight line represents God?"

Shebtai shrugged, as if what he thought was unimportant. "Could be." He offered his hand to Brittney, who still crouched in the trench that ran the length of the excavation site. She clutched her dental pick and brush in her left hand, gripped Shebtai's hand with her right, and climbed out of the trench.

"I must speak to you," Shebtai said seriously.

The others ceased their conversation and activity. Brittney smiled nervously.

"You have been given a demerit," he said softly, clasping her thin fingers between his rough, suntanned hands.

"What?" Brittney answered.

"Doran said you disobeyed curfew the other night," Shebtai said. He spoke quietly, in lullaby tones, but the others, standing just a few feet away, listened carefully.

"Doran? Who's Doran?"

"He is a soldier. He patrols Har Karkom at night."

Brittney had forgotten her nighttime walk, and the armed man who escorted her back to her tent.

"I didn't disobey curfew," she retorted. "I just went for a walk."

"When was this?" Jason asked.

"The other night," Brittney said, answering his question without turning her eyes away from Shebtai. "I can't believe this," she continued. "I didn't do anything wrong. I got stuffy in my tent. You mean I've got to be locked up like some kind of animal?"

Shebtai's tone was soothing. "It can be dangerous in the Negev after dark."

The memory of the creature that crossed her path on her walk slithered across Brittney's mind, but she shook it off and continued her speech of protest. "I ought to have the right to get a breath of fresh air when I can hardly breathe!"

Shebtai stroked his whiskered chin and watched her closely as she spoke.

"I can't believe you're doing this to me," she continued. "What difference does it make if I'm in my tent at 9:00 P.M. or 9:30?"

"Brittney," Jason said soothingly, hoping to be her knight in shining armor. "Don't sweat it. It's only one demerit."

"It's not the demerit, Jason," she countered. "It's just so silly. I didn't do anything wrong. They may be used to this stuffy weather out here but I'm not. I shouldn't have to be a prisoner in my own tent."

"Girl," Darcelle said in a kind tone, "we knew there would be rules, and we agreed to follow them while we were here."

"I understand what she's going through," Philip said. He thought of his father, and the many arguments they had. "She shouldn't be punished for getting some fresh air."

"She knew it was wrong," Bryan said matter-of-factly. "She just didn't care."

"Just get out of here with your holier-than-thou attitude," Brittney retorted. She had often wondered what it was she didn't like about Bryan; she suddenly realized it was the way he treated everyone, like he always had to be right and everyone else always had to be wrong.

Shebtai turned her to face the west, and pointed across the stark desert, toward the Israeli-Egyptian border, which lay less than ten miles away. "Do you know the story of the *Pesach?*"

"Huh?" Brittney looked up into his sparkling eyes, puzzlement mixing with the anger in her face. The others traded doubtful looks.

"You might call it 'Passover,'" he said. "The Hebrew people were slaves in Egypt, where they were cruelly oppressed."

"I feel like I'm back in Sunday school," Philip whispered to Jason.

"Shhh! I want to hear this," Jason responded.

"God sent plagues on the Egyptians, to humiliate their gods and persuade Pharaoh, the Egyptian ruler, to let the Hebrew people go. The tenth plague was the death of the firstborn; every firstborn son, from the son of the Pharaoh, to the son of the slave girl, to the firstborn of the cattle, would die at midnight. He promised them that there would be loud wailing throughout the land, worse than there had ever been before, and worse than there would ever be again." Shebtai's voice possessed a hushed quality, yet it was strong and unwavering.

He looked only at Brittney, as if everything and everyone around them had ceased to exist. Their faces were inches apart. "Then the God of the Hebrews issued some odd instructions. He told his people that the head of each household was to kill a spotless lamb, and smear its blood on the sides and tops of the doorframes of their homes."

He smiled warmly. "What a silly thing to do, eh?" His face became serious and his bushy gray eyebrows creased his forehead. "Yet everyone who obeyed God's instruction was saved from the horrible thing that happened that night. Only those who ignored God's command came to harm.

"The rules at Har Karkom are for your protection, Brittney," he continued. "There are many dangers in the Negev: scorpions and snakes and sudden storms—things more dangerous than a stuffy tent. The military's tanks and helicopters often conduct night maneuvers in the area. And it is important, too, that my volunteers do not fall asleep while they are swinging a pickax." He smiled in a fatherly sort of way. "Do you understand? The rules here are to give you the safest and most effective experience. They are not to make you a prisoner, but like God's commands, they are meant to protect you and provide good things for you."

His hand never left her shoulder as he spoke, and he embraced her, not like a boyfriend would, Brittney reflected, but as a father might—*any father except hers*, she figured. She felt flattered by Shebtai's concern, and her anger had long since dissipated in the warmth of his sincerity.

Brittney's expression softened. She looked from Shebtai to the others and smiled with embarrassment.

Shebtai clapped his hands and glanced at his watch. "So," he said, facing the group. "We must be getting back to camp." He gripped his belt, hitched his pants up over his midsection, and headed directly for the Land Rover.

Brittney fell into step with Darcelle, Jason, Philip, and Bryan, and followed Shebtai. She switched the dental pick and brush from her left hand to her right hand, and realized that she had not yet put them away in the chest that was kept on the other side of the excavation site, under a flimsy awning that also provided shade for rest periods. To put them away now would cause her to miss the ride back to camp with the others. It was only a fifteen-minute walk, but she quickly decided to save herself the trouble; she shoved the tools into her back hip pocket and climbed into the Land Rover for the trip back to camp.

☆   ☆   ☆

"Give me that thing!" Maury shouted at Ratsbane, yanking the keyboard to the mammoth control console out of his assistant's hands.

"What?" Ratsbane protested. "What's the problem? I had it going good."

Maury began rapidly typing, the claws on his turtle hands clacking against the keys like a secretary's painted fingernails.

"I've got that Brittney chick eating out of the palm of my hand," Ratsbane said. "Did you hear what she said? She's talking about *her* rights, and defending herself according to what *she* says is wrong."

"Perhaps," Maury countered without taking his eyes off the video screen. "But then you ruined it all by letting that graybeard tell one of his stories!"

Ratsbane turned one eye directly upon Maury. "What, that nonsense about the Passover? I don't see what you're getting so worked up about."

"The man is dangerous," Maury barked. "He says things about the Enemy and the Law that we don't want these humans to hear." He stared at the screen; Brittney sat between Jason and Darcelle in Shebtai's Land Rover. He punched one key hard a dozen times or more and then turned to look Ratsbane in the eye. "Never forget," Maury said viciously, "we aren't the only ones working behind the scenes up there."

☆   ☆   ☆

After they had washed and eaten lunch, Jason, Philip, Avi, Darcelle, and Brittney crowded into Shebtai's Land Rover for the long, hot drive to Mizpeh Ramon.

Darcelle turned to Philip, who had engineered the seating arrangements so that Avi not only sat with him but on his lap. She was just about to ask where Bryan was, when he appeared with a young, dark-haired girl.

"Is there room for us?" he asked cheerily. No one responded at first; they all stared dumbly at Bryan and his companion.

Jason finally broke the silence. "I'll sit back here with the laundry," he said. His tone was not happy; he did not want to surrender his cozy, crowded seat next to Brittney, but he scrambled over the backseat and settled atop the cloth laundry bags that occupied the thin space between the backdoor and the seat.

Bryan and the girl climbed into the vehicle and squeezed awkwardly into the space Jason had vacated. After the Land Rover lurched into motion, Avi hesitated a moment and then spoke.

"Everyone," she said, "this is Susan Arens. Her mother is one of the archaeologists on the staff here at Har Karkom."

The group introduced themselves to Susan. Darcelle asked where she was from, and Susan answered, in broken English, that she lived in Italy, where her parents were university professors. Brittney asked how old she was; Susan said she just turned fourteen.

Bryan's arrival with Susan made it seem to Brittney like everyone was pairing off. Philip and Avi seemed to be getting along well, and Bryan had found Susan somehow; watching the shy couples made her think of Matt and how they used to go everywhere together. When they first got together, it didn't matter what they did or where they went; even riding in a rickety Land Rover would have been fun. *It was so great to be in love,* she thought. So great that nothing else seemed important to her.

The noise and dust of the ride from the camp to High-way 40 discouraged conversation, but once they turned onto the two-lane paved road that wound the length of the Negev between the Wilderness of Paran and the Wilder-ness of Zin, Shebtai began to talk. He entertained them with a recitation of the contradictions and ironies that characterized modern-day Israel. He explained how the world's only Jewish state had been brought into existence, in the War for Independence in 1948, by Jewish settlers and immigrants who defeated better-armed and better-positioned Arab enemies.

"Father was a *sabra* who fought in the War for Independence," Avi explained proudly, pronouncing *sabra* to rhyme with *candelabra.*

"What's a *sabra?*" Darcelle asked.

"It is a Jew who was born in this land," Shebtai said. "I was Avi's age when I first fought for Israel." He pronounced Israel with three distinct syllables.

Shebtai went on to explain that Israel had always had to fight for survival, but had never lost territory in a war. The history of modern Israel, he said, was a history of strategic land being won militarily—and later returned diplomati-cally—to and from those who had attacked Israel and at-tempted to destroy it.

"Yet in Israel," he explained, "most Arabs and Jews live and work peacefully together."

"Why do we always hear about uprisings and terrorist attacks back home, then?" Brittney asked.

"A few do make it hard for the rest," he said. "But they are a few. Of course, reporters are not interested to hear about Jews and Arabs living together."

Shebtai pulled the Land Rover into the town and jerked to a stop at the curb. Slowly and awkwardly, the group extracted themselves from the vehicle and stood in front of the wide-open storefront of a tiny grocery. They stood on the curb stretching and shaking themselves, when suddenly the air was pierced by a mournful wail that seemed to come from everywhere at once.

"What is that?" Philip asked. "What's going on?"

"It sounds like someone's in pain!" Jason added.

"It's the call to prayer," Avi said. Her father stepped into the grocery store as the loud chanting continued. "It is the signal for all Muslims to stop whatever they are doing and perform their afternoon prayers."

The group stood in a tight cluster at one end of the little store and stared through a narrow doorway. Two men knelt on a colorful rug in the back room and touched their faces to the ground.

"What are they doing?" Bryan asked incredulously.

"They're praying," Brittney said, a note of exasperation in her voice.

"Yeah, but what about their store? What if I want to buy something?"

"You'll just have to wait until they're done."

"What if somebody comes along and steals something?"

"This is an Arab town, Bryan," Avi said. "Almost everyone is doing the same thing they're doing."

"It gives me the creeps," Bryan said loudly. He pointed at the kneeling forms of the storekeeper. "It's demonic—that's what it is." Several in the group tried unsuccessfully to quiet him as the man in the back of the store rose, folded his mat, and returned to the counter. "Can't you see that? He's bowing to a false god." He turned to the storekeeper. "I'm not buying anything in this store, I can tell you that. Some day every knee shall bow and every tongue confess that Jesus Christ is Lord!"

Shebtai was suddenly standing at Bryan's side. He smiled as he spoke, but there was no humor in his voice. "Israel is a nation of many religions," he said, speaking slowly and deliberately. "Jews, Christians, Muslims, and others all come to Israel because it is holy to their faith. We take our responsibility to honor and safeguard the practice of all religions very seriously. Any threat to the peace of one religion is a threat to the state of Israel. Do you understand what I am saying?" His voice was hard.

Bryan answered with a nod, his lips drawn tight across his face. He took Susan by the hand and led her out of the tiny store.

The group had the next hour and a half to spend in Mizpeh Ramon while waiting for the laundry to be done. They bought candy at the Arab grocery store, and discovered that the chocolate bars sold in Israel—even those bearing the names of American manufacturers—tasted nothing like the chocolate bars at home. They learned that the grocery store and an equally small meat market around the corner were the "supermarkets" of most Israeli towns. They watched a six- or seven-year-old boy herding three bleating sheep down the street toward the meat market.

Finally, Shebtai loaded the cloth bags into the Land Rover. Jason, still hoping to sit next to Brittney on the ride back to Har Karkom, waited for Philip or Bryan to offer to take his former position, but neither did so. He finally allowed Shebtai to help him into a position in the back that wouldn't mess up the sacks of laundry. The others returned to their cramped positions in the vehicle and returned to camp.

☆　☆　☆

"I wish I could strangle that meddlesome graybeard," Maury muttered.

Ratsbane had been playing with a sizable spider he had found scurrying across the floor of the laboratory, detaching the creature's legs one by one. Suddenly aware that Maury was speaking to him, Ratsbane popped the remains of the arachnid into his mouth and answered his mentor with a muffled "Hmmmm?"

"You must watch him closely, Ratsbane. He's a dangerous man." Maury punched a rapid series of keys, and the huge video screen before them arranged itself into five smaller screens focusing individually on Brittney, Darcelle, Jason, Philip, and Bryan. "You see, every one of those humans," Maury said, pointing at the screen with a stubby turtle finger, "must be told that it's up to them to decide what's right or what's wrong. I must convince every one of them that the decision about what's right or wrong must be based on their own standards, their own ideas."

"Yeah, yeah," Ratsbane squeaked, in a voice that resonated like the sound of fingernails on a blackboard. "I got that part. We've got to prevent them from looking to the Enemy as the moral standard, and instead prompt them to justify their attitudes and actions based on their own personal interests."

Maury constantly typed commands and coordinates into the control center as Ratsbane talked, turning and nodding when the ant-headed demon finished.

"Precisely!" he said, ignoring Ratsbane's mocking tone. "Because, if we can get them to believe that, it becomes child's play to convince them that since everyone must decide for himself what's right for him, they must therefore tolerate everyone else's view of what's right for them!"

Ratsbane's bulbous eyes blinked blankly. "Isn't that what the old guy was saying?"

"No, that's the problem!" Maury said. "Graybeard is kind toward people whose background or beliefs are different from his, but he believes nonetheless that some things are true for all people." Maury sighed with exasperation and pointed to Bryan's image on the screen. "We can't have that kind of tolerance. We must promote a twisted concept of tolerance. Why do you think I prompted this one to spout off the way he did outside that little grocery store?"

Ratsbane shrugged his frog shoulders. "Because it was fun," he answered.

"No! Because I'll be able to use it someday."

"How are you going to do that?" Ratsbane asked.

"You haven't learned anything about absolute truth, have you, ant-face?" He sighed with frustration. "Okay, OK, let me spell it out for you."

He poked a sharp turtle fingernail at Ratsbane's chest. "Once a human accepts the idea that truth is relative—that each person must determine what is right and wrong from within himself—our twisted concept of tolerance becomes an absolute must."

"An absolute?" asked Ratsbane.

"Absolutely," Maury answered vehemently. "Tolerance must become the human's *only* absolute truth."

"And that's good?" Ratsbane asked.

"No, that's not good," Maury retorted. "That's *great!* Such a twisted concept of tolerance will shake the very foundation of the Enemy's absolute truth. Because, you see, if they believe that what's right for them may not be right for someone else, they absolutely have to be tolerant of every imaginable behavior! Otherwise, their position makes no sense."

"But it makes no sense anyway," Ratsbane countered. "And besides, how are you going to transform the virtue of tolerance into a twisted concept?"

Maury stepped away from the console and began pacing. "Tolerance, I admit, is generally a human virtue, when it opens human minds to new ideas and prevents them from judging one another like graybeard was carrying on about. Because, as you know, there is only one absolute judge—our Enemy, the Holy One."

Ratsbane let out a groan as if someone had gouged him. Maury went on.

"But, remember, I said before that if humans reject the Holy One as the Absolute Judge and accept truth as subjective, they set themselves up as lord and judge in His place. They become their own gods."

"Won't they see through that?" Ratsbane asked.

"It worked with Eve, didn't it?" Maury retorted. "And anyway, we don't let them see the implications of their actions.

And preserving the human right to determine what is truth will be seen as the highest form of virtue—even though it rejects the only truth that is absolute, the truth of the Enemy."

"So-o-o-o," Ratsbane began slowly punctuating each word, "if our twisted concept of tolerance is going to undermine the Enemy's absolute truth, humans must be *intolerant* of anyone who asserts that they believe in absolute truth."

"Praise be to Satan, he's got it!" proclaimed Maury. "That's why Bryan's intolerance will come in handy later on," he continued. "Tolerance must be proclaimed as the only absolute virtue and then we must get them to condemn anyone who asserts any other absolute truth!"

"So," Ratsbane interjected, "the more we can get people like Bryan to be extreme, judgmental, and condemning, the more our twisted concept of tolerance is seen as a virtue."

"You are a foul and contemptible wretch, Ratsbane," proclaimed Maury.

Ratsbane took one step back and bowed slightly. "Thank you, Maury. Thank you very much."

The Inside Story: Truth and Tolerance

Demon Maury's strategy is truly diabolical . . . and many adults and students have fallen for it.

It sounds so good. Our society proudly states that everyone has the right to decide what is right and wrong for themselves. "Religion, you know, is a personal and private matter. And when someone decides what truth is right, everyone should respect that choice. No one should be allowed to impose his own idea of truth on another."

This concept of tolerance has arisen in our culture as a new cardinal virtue. It has become synonymous with goodness and open-mindedness; intolerance has come to connote bigotry.

The problem is that many misrepresent the concept of tolerance—it has become a truth laced with error. But the correct concept of tolerance is virtuous because it prompts us to give due consideration to those whose practices differ from our own—it requires us to be courteous and kind to someone who doesn't view things just like we do. And Maury is right when he says, "tolerance is to help keep each of us from judging the other." Why? Because God is the only Perfect One capable of judging righteously. Scripture makes it clear that we are not to judge, but to leave such things in God's hands (see Rom. 14:10–13 and Ps. 9:3–10).

However, because we are not to pass judgment on another does not change the fact that truth is absolute. Tolerance was meant to guard our attitudes—it was not meant to be twisted into a cultural "law" that proclaims right and wrong as a matter of individual preference. There is nothing virtuous about condoning another person's view that is clearly in violation of God's absolute commands.

God has given all of us the freedom to accept or reject Him, as well as the freedom to accept or reject His truth. Consequently, we must remember that when a person rejects God's absolute truth, they are rejecting Him, not us. It is God's job to judge. It is our job to live according to His truth, and to share that truth in love and compassion.

6

Trouble in Brittney's Tent

Later that evening, Jason stepped into Brittney and Darcelle's tent. Brittney stood beside her cot, lighting the lamp on the crate between the beds; Darcelle's cot was empty.

"Are you decent?" Jason asked.

"Hi, Jason," Brittney answered, scooping the dental pick and brush off her cot where she had tossed them earlier that day. She set the tools on the crate between the beds. "Come on in."

"Avi said she'd take us swimming after dinner tomorrow. Are you in?"

"Yeah," she said with a shrug. "That sounds great."

Jason was surprised by her tone. He cocked his head and examined her face. "What's wrong?" he asked softly.

Brittney met his searching gaze with tearful eyes. She flopped down on the edge of her cot and rubbed her eyes with the thumb and fingers of her left hand. She started talking without moving her hands away from her closed eyes.

"It's not working," she said with a heavy sigh.

"What?" he asked. "What's not working?"

"My whole reason for coming here," she explained, "was to get away from Matt."

Good, Jason thought. *I like that plan.*

"But I can't stop thinking about him."

Jason swallowed. That really wasn't what he wanted to hear. And he knew his next question wasn't really what he wanted to ask. "Why did you want to get away from Matt?"

She dropped her hand to her lap, opened her eyes, and looked at Jason, who still stood at the end of her cot. "You don't want to know," she said, swallowing hard to control her tears.

He sat down beside her, close to her, on the cot. He picked her right hand off her lap and held it. "Yeah, I do," he said, telling himself all along that he was crazy. He should be sweeping her off her feet, not helping her fix things up with Matt. *What's wrong with me?* he thought. *Matt's a million miles away, and I'm right here. Why can't she forget about him and notice me?*

Despite his internal agony, Jason listened as Brittney poured out all that she and Matt had done, all that she regretted, yet all that she now missed.

"I know that what we did was wrong," she said, not at all sure she was telling the truth. "But I don't know *where* I went wrong. I mean, I want the closeness that Matt and I had, yet I don't want to do . . . you know . . . the other stuff any more. Her throat tightened around her last words and she fought for control.

Jason's stomach knotted at the misery he read on her face. He wished he could kiss her pain and make it go away. "Look, Brittney—you can't change the past," he said, in a pleading, urgent tone. "None of us can. But you can start a new relationship out on the right track. You just have to find the right guy—a Christian guy who can help you *stay,* you know, pure." He squeezed her hand, hoping she'd recognize just who that guy was.

"You must think I'm terrible," she said. "I can't believe I told you all this."

Jason shook his head and draped an arm around her shoulders. He stifled the surge of excitement his action caused and spoke softly to her. "Brittney, I—" *I love you,* he wanted to say. *I want you to forget Matt and give me a chance.* "I don't think you're terrible at all," he said instead.

"You're a good friend, Jason, a good Christian friend. Maybe that's the big problem—Matt's not a good Christian like you," she said, wiping tears from her eyes. He cringed at her words. They stood, and embraced. Jason held her tight, wishing that she could embrace him the way he was holding her.

Suddenly, Shebtai's voice sounded outside her tent, asking for permission to come in. She and Jason separated, and looked at each other with guilt written on their faces. In an awful instant of realization, they each suddenly remembered that boys were not allowed in girls tents. After a few moments of hopeless silence, Brittney called to the dig director to come in.

He entered through the tent flap. "I am sorry to interrupt your conversation," he said. He addressed himself to Jason. "But I must ask you to please leave this young woman's tent."

"I guess this means a demerit?" Jason asked.

The man nodded. "As does that," he added, pointing to the digging tools in full view of everyone on the crate beside Brittney's bed. "Do they belong to you?" he asked Jason.

"No—they're not mine," Jason said.

Brittney glanced at the brush and pick. Her mouth opened, but her words of defense merged into a helpless sigh. "They're mine," she said, "I'm sorry, Shebtai. I'm really sorry."

"I am sorry too," he said. "But there are good reasons for the rules." His expression communicated concern, not anger. "Do you understand?"

Shebtai motioned, and Jason muttered a few words of encouragement and farewell to Brittney before ducking through the flap and out of the tent.

Brittney flopped down on the cot again and shot a look at the tools beside her bed. "I understand everything you said this morning about the curfew and everything . . . I just have a hard time obeying all these rules I don't understand."

She raised both hands and tucked her hair behind her ears. "You and Avi may be used to all these rules, but I'm not. Like, Avi was telling us how you have to even use two different sets of silverware. I just don't see the point."

Shebtai smiled. He sat on Darcelle's cot and faced Brittney.

"You are right," he said, his eyes flickering in the lamplight like twin fireflies, "it is easier to obey rules you understand. The reasons behind the rules are important. But there is something even more important than that."

He drew a deep breath, and stroked his gray-and-black beard with his thumb and forefinger. "When God gave the Law to my people many centuries ago," he said, "He gave us 613 commands and rules about how we should live, what we should eat, and how we should treat other people. Many of those rules may seem silly, like not mixing certain fabrics together, keeping certain silverware separate, or not yoking different animals together.

"But there was a reason behind every one of those rules, an important principle. For example, the purpose of the hundreds of laws separating clean from unclean, good from bad, one kind from another kind, was to give Israel a lesson in purity. Whether or not we understood every one of those laws was not so important; what was important was that they communicated to us that purity was an important value. All those laws told us clearly that God values purity.

"But there is even something more important than that, Brittney," he said. He leaned toward her as if he were preparing to leap from his position.

"Because God did not give the Law just to teach us what we should do and what we should not do; it was given to reveal the very nature and character of God Himself to His people. The Law—"You shall not kill," "You shall not steal," "You shall not lie"—shows us *what God is like*. And all those regulations about food and fabric communicate that purity is right because God Himself is pure. I do not have to wonder whether this action is right or that action is wrong, because if something is like God, it is right; if it is not like Him, it is wrong."

Brittney looked at Shebtai with a blank expression.

"Yeah, well, I can see how that would be important for you, because you're Jewish. But what's it got to do with me?"

"Everything!" bellowed Shebtai. "It has *everything* to do with you, because you cannot enjoy God's protection and provision if your actions do not reflect His nature and character."

She blinked at him, uncomprehendingly.

He folded one arm under the other and stroked his beard. "You hope to be married some day, do you not?"

She nodded.

"Has God given commands about love and sex and marriage?"

She nodded again.

"Right. He has said, 'You shall not commit adultery.' Why,—because He wants to spoil our fun? No, because the love of a husband and wife should be pure—that is, free of contamination—and it should be faithful—reserved only for each other. That is God's standard for you because that is what He is like. He is pure, and faithful, and He wants you to know the kind of trust and intimacy that can thrive in that kind of a relationship."

Brittney found herself blushing. *Had Shebtai heard her conversation with Jason? Did he know about her?*

"You see, Brittney, God's commands are not intended to spoil our fun or to frustrate us," he said, his voice softening. "They are meant to reflect *Him*, and to enrich us."

She nodded. Moisture began to rise in her eyes again. She looked into Shebtai's face and saw understanding and compassion there. They both stood, and he embraced her as she cried.

☆   ☆   ☆

"No!" Maury stood before the mammoth computer console and video screen in the RAID laboratory, screaming and stomping his feet like a temperamental two-year-old who's just dropped an ice cream cone. "No! No! No!"

"You can stop screaming in my ears any time, now," Ratsbane growled as he tapped the keyboard and watched the screen.

"You don't *have* ears, you worthless insect!"

"I have them; you just can't see—"

"Never mind that, you've ruined it—you've ruined *everything* with your incompetence!"

Ratsbane looked at the screen. "I don't see what the big deal is. All I have to do is—"

"All you have to do is put the cat back in the bag," Maury screamed, his spectacles bouncing around on his turtle nose like a cowboy on a bronco. "*Can* you do that?"

"Put the cat back in the bag?" Ratsbane scratched the slick dome of his ant-head. "What are you talking about? What cat?"

"You let the old geezer let the cat out of the bag, you moronic boob! You let him spill the beans! You let him blow the lid off!"

"Huh?" The ebony depths of Ratsbane's eyes were as blank as the sockets of a Halloween mask.

Maury glared at Ratsbane through his black-framed glasses. He straightened himself and stretched his neck far out of the shell that clung to his back. He opened his turtle beak in a vicious snarl. "Our whole strategy," he said, "will collapse if these detestable humans see where absolute truth truly comes from. We'll be hamstrung if they begin to understand that truth proceeds, not from their opinion, but from the person of the Enemy Himself."

"Oh, we can let them judge their actions and attitudes by their own ideas; we can even let them compare their actions to each other . . . but once they see how truth flows from the Enemy the way light glows from a candle, we . . . are . . . sunk!"

Ratsbane's mandibles spread apart into a grimace. His neck expanded with a loud gulp. "What are we going to do?" he asked miserably.

"Move over," Maury ordered, pushing his glasses up his nose and stepping to the computer keyboard. "Do exactly what I tell you."

The Inside Story: The Steps of Truth

Brittney Marsh has been struggling to sort right from wrong in her relationship with Matt. She's been trying to figure out what will bring her happiness and fulfillment. But she's been trying to determine all that on her own; she's like a baseball player who faces the opposing pitcher without a bat. And she's been striking out.

There is an answer for Brittney. There are four simple, but not necessarily easy, steps she must take. In fact, these four steps are necessary for each of us if we want to make right choices in life. We might call them "The Four Cs of Right Choices:"

1. **Consider** the choice;
2. **Compare** it to God;
3. **Commit** to God's way; and
4. **Count** on God's protection and provision.

CONSIDER THE CHOICE. Brittney made a tough choice in her relationship with Matt when she broke up with him. But long before she broke up, she made a number of "little," almost imperceivable choices. When she began dating Matt, who was an unbeliever, she made a choice. Where they went on dates involved more choices. When Matt first kissed her she made a choice. And when their kissing went much further she made yet another choice.

Looking back on it, Brittney didn't consider the little choices as individual crossroads that led her down the wrong path. But the first step in making the right choices in life, for Brittney and all of us, is to consider each choice as potentially being a right choice or a wrong choice, not according to what *she* thinks, but according to an objective standard of right and wrong.

COMPARE IT TO GOD. How, then, can we know whether a specific action or attitude is right or wrong? By comparing it to God. He—and He alone—determines whether something is right or wrong.

Suppose you and I had a dispute about who was right and who was wrong about a length of wood I had cut for you. I measured it and told you it was one meter long; you measured it with your own meterstick and pronounced that it was less than one meter. How could we determine who was right? We could take a vote. We could flip a coin. Or, we could appeal to an absolute standard of measurement.

And it so happens that there exists an absolute standard for such measurements—in Sevres, France, at the headquarters of the International Bureau of Weights and Measures. That bureau establishes and guards the international standards for metric measurements. To know the truth we need only put the object in question to the test by comparing it to the original—the standard.

Webster defines *truth* as "fidelity to an original or standard." As we must do when measuring meters, we must also do in discerning right from wrong; to determine moral truth, we must ask: How does it compare to the original, to *the standard?* And, Maury knew that if Brittney compared her actions to the standard of God Himself, she would know the truth.

The very reason we have this concept that some things are right and some things are wrong is because there exists a Creator, Jehovah God, and He is a righteous God. The reason we think that there are such things as "fair" and "unfair" is because our Maker is a just God. The reason love is a virtue and hatred a vice is because the God who formed us is a God of love. The reason honesty is right and deceit is wrong is because God is true. The reason chastity is moral and promiscuity is immoral is because God is pure.

It is God and God alone who determines absolute truth; He defines what is right **for all people, for all places, for all times.** But absolute truth is not something God decides; it is something He is. Such truth is objective because God exists outside ourselves; it is universal because God is above all; it is constant because God is eternal. Absolute truth is absolute because it originates from the original—the Standard.

Therefore, if Brittney sincerely wants to determine whether what she and Matt were doing was right (after all, they loved each other, remember?), she must compare it to God. But how?

If you and I had a physics assignment to determine whether rolling friction slows an object faster than sliding friction, how would we decide? We would construct a test. For example, we might get into your car, drive thirty-five miles per hour across an empty parking lot and, at a predetermined point, slam on the brake pedal so that the brakes lock and we slide to a stop. Then we might return to the starting point, accelerate to thirty-five miles per hour again and, at the same point, apply the brake as hard as possible while keeping the wheels rolling. By comparing the distance the vehicle traveled before stopping each time, we would learn that rolling friction stops an object faster than sliding friction.

But what kind of comparison can we make to determine whether "sex between two people who love each other" is right or wrong? We can follow the same pattern God Himself has used to communicate truth to men and women throughout history. God began His revelation of right and wrong with the Ten Commandments (actually, He began with one command—"you must not eat from the tree of the knowledge of good and evil"). We can compare our attitudes

and actions to God's commands—His *precepts*—that is, what
He has spoken to us, and His spoken Word (the Scriptures)
point to universal moral principles which, in turn, spring from
the Person of God Himself—His very nature and character.

PRECEPT

Few people realize that a precept—the rules, the
regulations, the laws in Scripture—is but the first step in
understanding basic morality. In biblical terms, for example, sexual immorality is all extramarital (including
premarital) sex. God has spoken through the law, and He
has made His standard clear: sexual involvement outside
of marriage is wrong.

The precept is clear:

"Abstain from . . . sexual immorality" (Acts 15:29).

"Flee from sexual immorality" (1 Cor. 6:18).

"We should not commit sexual immorality" (1 Cor. 10:8).

"But among you there must not be even a hint of sexual
immorality . . . because these are improper for God's holy
people" (Eph. 5:3).

"Put to death, therefore, whatever belongs to your earthly
nature: sexual immorality [and] impurity . . . " (Col. 3:5).

"It is God's will that you . . . should avoid sexual immorality" (1 Thess. 4:3).

But the law or precepts of the Lord do not only serve as
a long list of dos and don'ts that define right and wrong in
explicit terms. They also point to larger moral principles. The
Bible tells us that the law leads us by the hand, like a child
going to school, to learn deeper lessons.

PRINCIPLE

A principle is a norm or standard that may be applied
to more than one type of situation. To understand the difference between a principle and a precept, think of a principle

as expressing the fundamental truth on which a precept is based. Principles help explain the "why" behind a precept or command.

God's law forbidding sexual immorality is not predicated on a desire to squelch Brittney's freedom or squash her fun. The "negative" command expresses a positive principle. In fact, the biblical command to "flee sexual immorality" is based on at least three positive principles: love, purity, and faithfulness.

The biblical standard of sex is one of love:
For the commandments, "You shall not commit adultery," "You shall not murder," "You shall not steal," "You shall not bear false witness," "You shall not covet," and if there is any other commandment, are all summed up in this saying, namely, "You shall love your neighbor as yourself." Love does no harm to a neighbor; therefore love is the fulfillment of the law (Rom. 13:9-10, NKJV).

According to the Bible, love is evident when the happiness, health, and spiritual growth of another person is as important to you as your own. When the Word of God records the command, "Love your neighbor as yourself," it doesn't command us to love our neighbor more than ourselves. We are to love God more than we love ourselves, but we are to love our neighbor as we love ourselves.

The problem, however, is that Brittney is working from a faulty concept of love. In her mind, love is definitely the greatest determining factor in the decision to engage in sex. She believed that her love for Matt made sexual involvement OK; because she loved him, she reasoned, it was right to express that love sexually. Her mistake was in accepting a contemporary counterfeit of "true love." True love, as defined by God, sets clear boundaries for sex. The principle of true love requires that the happiness, health, and spiritual growth of another person be as important to us as our own before love makes sex right.

When I speak I often tell the audience that I believe "love makes it right." That statement is invariably greeted with strange looks, especially on the adult faces in the audience. So I go on quickly to clarify the principle of "true love."

"Do you," I say, "expect true love to produce intimacy? Do you expect it to result in a closeness and connectedness, a bonding of two people?"

The crowd inevitably responds with nods of approval.

"Do you," I continue, "expect true love to be giving, and trusting—a love that wraps its arms around you and says, 'No matter what, I will love you?'"

Again, heads will nod, and students will smile warmly in agreement.

"Do you," I proceed, "envision true love to be secure and safe, loyal, and forever?"

Without exception, crowds will agree to that principle of "true love." Well, for love to be like that it needs a boundary of solid protection and provision.

Ephesians 5:28 (NKJV) helps us understand the biblical principle of love even better: "So husbands ought to love their own wives as their own bodies; he who loves his wife loves himself." What does it mean to love our own body as Scripture commands? The next verse explains: "For no one ever hated his own flesh, but nourishes and cherishes it, just as the Lord does the church" (emphasis added). The word *nourish* means "to provide for" and *cherish* means "to protect."

You see, God's principle of love means to provide for and protect the happiness, health, and spiritual growth of another person as much as you do your own happiness, health, and spiritual growth.

The biblical standard of sex is one of purity: "Marriage should be honored by all, and the marriage bed kept pure, for God will judge the adulterer and all the sexually immoral" (Heb. 13:4). God's standard of sex demands that the sexual relationship be kept pure and beautiful. God designed sex to be enjoyed in a husband-wife relationship, for procreation (Gen. 1:28), for spiritual unity (Gen. 2:24), and for recreation (Prov. 5:18-19). It's meant to form an unbroken

circle, a pure union: two virgins entering an exclusive relationship. That circle, that union, can be broken even before marriage, if one or both of the partners has not kept
the marriage bed pure by waiting to have sex until it can
be done in the purity of a husband-wife relationship.

The biblical standard of sex is also one of faithfulness. "Love
and faithfulness meet together," the Bible says (Ps. 85:10). In
practical terms, this means that the biblical standard of sex
requires a commitment of two people to remain faithful to
each other. If the act of love is to produce the emotional,
physical, and spiritual intimacy that Brittney desires, it must
be committed, it must be faithful. That is why marriage is
central to biblical sexuality, because it binds two people together in a lifelong commitment.

During my speaking tours I often ask this question of the
guys who are hosting me on a university campus or when
speaking at a church: "Are you staying faithful to your wife?"
The single guys will respond, "I'm not married, Josh." Then I
point out that you don't have to be married to stay faithful to
your future mate. The lifelong commitment to be sexually pure
to your mate requires faithfulness before you ever meet them.

God's precepts regarding human sexuality are grounded
upon the principles of biblical love, purity, and faithfulness.
Those principles, in turn, reflect the person of God Himself.

PERSON

To know what we believe about God's precepts (and
even the principles of truth that lie behind those precepts),
and not know the Person from whom they derive, is worthless. Bryan, for example, knows what God's law says, but he
doesn't see its extensions—what it teaches us about the character of God. The ultimate purpose of God in every precept
is to bring people to the knowledge of Himself.

Shebtai understands this progression. His stories and
explanations of the Jewish ceremonies and laws reveals

something about the character of God. The Bible says that, after God spoke to Moses "face to face, as a man speaks with his friend" (Exod. 33:11), Moses prayed, "If you are pleased with me, teach me your ways *so I may know you* . . . " (see Exod. 33:13, my emphasis). Learning God's ways—understanding His laws and the principles behind them—acquaints us with the person of God Himself.

Shebtai's obedience to all the details of Jewish regulations concerning dress, food preparation and consumption, the forms of worship, and so on, constantly reminds him of what God is like. To him, the prescriptions, instructions, and codes of God's Law offer important insights into the mystery of the eternal Creator and why He has given us His Law.

God's law is not an end in itself. Some of His commands were illustrative, others were practical, but all were—and are—an expression of His character. King David acknowledged,

> The law of the Lord is perfect,
> reviving the soul.
> The statutes of the Lord are trustworthy,
> making wise the simple.
> The precepts of the Lord are right,
> giving joy to the heart.
> The commands of the Lord are radiant,
> giving light to the eyes.
> The fear of the Lord is pure,
> enduring forever.
> The ordinances of the Lord are sure,
> and altogether righteous.

—Psalm 19:7-9

Note carefully the words David used to describe God's law: perfect, sure, right, radiant, pure, and righteous. Why do you think the law possesses those qualities? Because they are qualities that belong to the Lawgiver—God Himself. You see, ultimately, the truth does not reside in the commands; it resides in God. The truth would not cease being true if the Law were to disappear from the face of the earth, nor would it cease to be true if there were no humans to discern the principle—because the truth resides in the person of God Himself, who is eternal.

The principles of love, purity, and faithfulness then are right because they are from God—they reflect His nature and character. We are to compare our attitudes and actions to Him—the "original."

God is love. "The one who does not love does not know God, for God is love. By this the love of God was manifested in us, that God has sent his only begotten Son into the world so that we might live through Him" (1 John 4:8-9, NASB). Love is not simply what God does; it is who He is. And by His nature, He views the happiness, health, and spiritual growth of others more important than Himself. That is what motivated Him to send His own Son to suffer and die for us. God's kind of love always protects and provides for us.

God is pure. "Everyone who has this hope [of glory] in him purifies himself, just as he [God] is pure" (1 John 3:3). God has continually strived to communicate His purity to His people: He demanded the use of pure gold in the construction of the tabernacle; He prescribed pure incense for use in worship; He required pure animals for sacrifice; He commanded pure hearts (see Matt. 5:8), pure religion (see James 1:27), and pure relationships (see 1 Tim. 5:2). As the prophet Habakkuk said, God's purity is such that even "[his] eyes are too pure to look on evil" (Hab. 1:13).

God is faithful. "Know therefore that the Lord your God is God," Moses told the Israelites. "He is the faithful God, keeping his covenant of love to a thousand generations of those who love him and keep his commands" (Deut. 7:9). Now that's faithfulness! God keeps His covenant to a thousand generations. As Paul told Timothy, even "if we are faithless, He remains faithful, for He cannot deny Himself" (2 Tim. 2:13, NASB). In other words, God cannot be unfaithful, because faithfulness is not something He does; it is something He is. He cannot "deny Himself;" He cannot contradict His own nature; He cannot be something other than what He is.

The virtue of chastity—biblical love, sexual purity, and faithfulness—is grounded in the nature and character of God. Brittney is only beginning to understand how her relationship with Matt contradicted God's character. Their sexual relationship was not loving, because they were not considering each other's happiness, health, and spiritual growth as important as their own. Their sexual involvement was not pure, because it was not being enjoyed in the context for which God designed it. It did not fit God's standard of faithfulness either, because it existed outside the lifelong, exclusive commitment of marriage.

Her sexual activity, then, was wrong, not simply because her parents disagreed with her, or because her youth group leader would have said it was wrong, but because she violated God's declaration that sex was to be enjoyed within the confines of a loving, faithful, and pure relationship of marriage.

We can then say that chastity—biblical love, sexual purity, and marital fidelity—is right **for all people, for all times, for all places.**

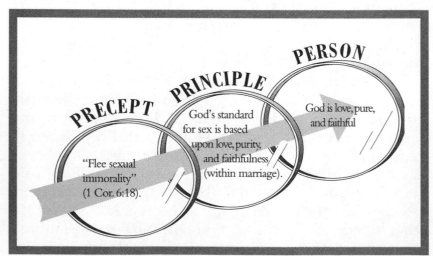

Brittney could have realized that what she was doing with Matt was wrong if first she would have **considered** each individual choice as potentially a choice between what is objectively right or wrong, independent of her own feelings or opinions, by **comparing** her attitude and action to God.

But recognizing a choice as absolutely right or wrong isn't all we need to know. There are two more vitally important steps we need to take.

7

The Water Hole at Wadi Ideid

Jason stood in the gathering summer dusk of Thursday evening and called to Brittney from outside her tent.

"Come on in," Brittney answered.

"Oh, no you don't," Jason said with a smile in his voice. "I'm waiting right here. Doran could be anywhere."

Brittney appeared quickly in the door of the tent.

"You're coming, aren't you?" he said.

"Yeah," she answered. "I've got my swimsuit on under my clothes. What time are we leaving?"

"Avi told Philip we'll meet at eight-fifteen behind the mess tent. That's less than a half-hour from now. Is Darcelle coming?"

"No, she said she wants to stay in and write some letters."

"Yeah, I should probably do that too." He paused. "But I'm not. Have you seen Bryan lately?"

"No, why?"

Jason shrugged. "I guess it's just you, me, Philip, and Avi, then." *Just two couples,* he thought. *Perfect.*

"Okay," Brittney said. "I'll see you at eight-fifteen."

Philip and Jason were already waiting behind the mess tent when Brittney arrived. The boys wore shorts, T-shirts, and tennis shoes without socks. Brittney was fully dressed over her one-piece swimsuit. Avi arrived soon after Brittney, wearing a dark two-piece suit with a towel draped over her shoulders. She wielded a battered flashlight with a lamp the size of the headlight on a car.

"Be quiet," Avi warned, switching the flashlight on, then off, to check the light. "We have to pass many tents as we go out of camp, so no talking until I say it is safe."

They made it out of camp without arousing notice, then descended the mountain as the sun disappeared in the western sky. Every stone, every prominence in the vast desert below seemed etched in sharp shadows. As they carefully navigated the steep path from the camp, Brittney pointed to a single, large stone standing along the path.

"That's the second one I've seen," she said, pointing to the somewhat rectangular rock standing on its narrow end. She turned to Avi. "What is it?"

Avi didn't break stride, but responded to Brittney in the gathering darkness. "It's a *menhir*," she said. "Father says they've probably been standing there for four thousand years or more." "What is it," Brittney repeated, "just a rock? It looks like it was put there for a reason."

"It was," Avi began, but Jason interrupted her.

"Yeah, there used to be a sign on one side, saying 'Next rest area five hundred miles.'"

"Father thinks these *menhirs* were places where people stopped on their way to Har Karkom. They were probably places set aside for resting and praying."

"Wait a minute," Jason said. The group stopped in the waning light of the evening. "You just reminded me. Your father stopped in the middle of nowhere when he was bringing us here from the airport and walked away from the car, stood there for a while, and then got back in the car without saying anything. Do you know what that was all about?"

Avi nodded seriously. "It is where a friend died in the six-day war. Father was with him. And ever since, whenever he passes that place he remembers his friend with a prayer."

They resumed their walk again, in silence at first. Darkness began to fall as they walked toward the water hole; a full moon lit their way, shedding an eerie light around them. Jason walked beside Brittney and occasionally placed a hand on her arm or shoulder as they walked around rocks or through a dry gully. It was exciting simply to touch her, and he noted happily that she did not shy from his touch.

He watched Brittney closely as they walked, pained at his inability to steer their relationship down a different path, but reminding himself that they had five more weeks in Israel. The longer she was away from Matt and the more she was around him, the greater his chances would be of slipping into the void left by her breakup with Matt.

He tried to picture him and Brittney together, holding hands, laughing, kissing. He wished he could tell her right now how he felt about her, but he reminded himself to be patient. *Five weeks is a long time*, he told himself again. *Anything can happen.*

Avi switched the flashlight on and led the way below the cliffs in the western valley at the foot of the mountain. "These water holes—they are called *gevim* in Hebrew—are fed by Wadi Ideid, a stream bed that comes and goes with the rains. But the water collects in pools and because the rock around it is so hard, it stays in the water hole, even during long periods of no rain."

"Is this an oasis we're going to?" Philip asked.

"No, only a water hole. An oasis has more water and more things growing. We are almost there now."

"How did you know about this place?" Philip asked.

"Father showed it to me two or three summers ago. He told me never to come here without him. But this is the first time I've had anyone but him to come with me."

Philip grunted. "All I can say is, I feel for you," he said. He gripped her hand and held it as they walked.

"What do you mean?"

"I know what it's like. My dad's real big on rules, just like yours. I know how crummy it can be to have to live with a father who's always telling you what you *can't* do and

where you *can't* go and who you *can't* hang around with."
He squeezed her hand and flashed her a sympathetic glance.
"Believe me, I know *just* what you're going through."

Avi's face spread into a smile, and she looked at him as
they walked carefully through a dry stream bed. "Father is not
like that at all!" she said. "I know my father loves me, and I
love him too. And I would not want him to be different.

"Since my mother died, he has had to try to raise a girl
by himself, and maybe he has not done everything right. But
I have always known that the reason he tells me rules is to
give me good things and keep me from bad things. He always tells me that, but I think I would know it anyway." She
craned her neck to look into Philip's face as they walked.
"You do not think your father's rules are good?"

Philip shrugged and grunted. He appeared to concen-
trate on the path ahead. "I wish I could say those things
about my father," he said.

Jason suddenly appeared at Philip's side and whispered
in Philip's ear as they walked awkwardly together. He then
jogged back to Brittney's side and watched as Philip spoke
softly to Avi.

"What was that all about?" Brittney asked.

"Oh, nothing," Jason answered nonchalantly.

The next moment, they arrived at the water hole. Brittney
sat on the rocky soil at the water's edge and began untying her
shoes. Philip and Jason flipped their shoes off, removed their
shirts, and went bounding wildly into the water.

Brittney felt a tiny giggle rise in her throat as she
watched Jason and Philip.

This is going to be fun, she thought.

It had been a long time since she had just had fun with
a boy; she and Matt had experienced very little besides passion and guilt in the past few months.

"Do you want me to wait for you?" Avi asked.

"No, you go ahead," Brittney said with a smile. "This
shoestring has a knot in it. I'll just be a minute."

Avi removed her shoes and splashed into the water. She swam to Philip and Jason, who screamed and splashed like children on the first day of summer camp.

Brittney had just untangled the knot in her shoestring when Jason called to her. She looked out into the water.

Her three friends stood side by side in water that reached just below their shoulders. Each of them held an object aloft in their hands. Brittney tried to peer through the darkness at her friends' forms.

"Come on in," Jason shouted. "Shed the suit! We're skinny dipping!" They waved the clothes they held in their hands and laughed.

Brittney's mouth dropped open, and despite the fact that there was no one near enough to see, she blushed a deep red. She tried to focus her eyes through the darkness. They couldn't be serious!

"Come on," they shouted. "We're waiting!"

Brittney looked at the shoes they had all left behind, lying beside her on the rocky soil. Suddenly she re-tied her shoes, stood, and began to run back the way they had all come.

"Brittney!" Jason shouted. He saw her begin to trot away from them, back toward camp. He lowered his hand, which gripped his T-shirt, and turned to Avi, who held her towel in the air. "What's she doing?"

Philip, who had also been waving his T-shirt in the air as part of the prank Jason had concocted, answered. "She's freaked. She's running back to camp."

"No!" Jason shouted. He looked from Philip to Avi. "She wouldn't do that. Would she?"

"What did you expect her to do, throw her clothes off and swim naked?" Philip asked.

"No!" he shouted. "Of course not. I just thought we'd play around for a few seconds, and then tell her it was a joke. I didn't expect her to go running off."

Jason screamed Brittney's name again and began to swim frantically toward the shore. Avi and Philip followed. They splashed ashore and fumbled in the moonlight, between a scraggly bush and a large boulder, to slip their shoes onto dripping wet feet.

"Come on," Jason said impatiently, "we're losing her." He kicked himself inwardly. This evening had been the perfect chance to start changing things between him and Brittney, and he'd blown it—as usual. He realized with a sudden pain that she had told him she was trying to end a relationship that had become too physical, and now she thought Jason had tried to get her to jump naked into a pond with him! He felt sick, and wished there was a way to erase the events of the last ten minutes.

"Hold on a minute—I can't get my shoe on." Philip hopped on one foot, and finally rested a hand on Avi's arm to balance himself.

"We'll never find Brittney now," Jason said. "Do you still have the flashlight?"

"It's around here somewhere." She peered carefully at the dark ground, and stepped over toward the large round rock opposite the bush. A moment later she switched the light on.

"At least we have a light," Philip said.

"Yeah," Jason countered. "But Brittney doesn't."

An embarrassed Brittney ran from the water hole and retraced the way the group had come.

I can't believe them, she thought. *No one said anything about skinny dipping.*

The moonlight cast sharp shadows along her way, and she wondered why the path didn't seem as treacherous on the way to the water hole as it did now. She began to pant from the exertion of climbing the slope back toward camp.

"I can't believe them," she said aloud. The sound of her voice seemed somehow reassuring in the strange darkness of the desert. "Jason's done some crazy things, but I can't believe he'd do that. It's just not right; they must *know* it's not right!"

She stopped. Something moved. She heard a sound, as if someone or something had kicked a stone or two. Something had moved out there, in the darkness, in the night. She strained to see into the shadows cast by the rocks and boulders that stood here and there on the pebbled desert floor. She had no idea what kind of animals lived in this harsh land; she remembered the thing that had slithered across her path a few nights ago in camp, and wished that she was back in her tent, sleeping peacefully.

She struggled to control her breathing. She listened carefully. Finally, she licked her lips and began walking briskly along the path.

Suddenly she stopped again. She had heard another noise, only it wasn't an animal kind of sound. She froze and held her breath for what seemed to be ten minutes until her breath burst out of her; she gulped for air and listened again.

Finally she identified the sound. It came from ahead of her on the trail, maybe off to her right a little bit. It was a muffled voice, a whisper. She inched her way carefully toward the sound, forgetting the darkness and danger that had controlled her thoughts just moments before. The path rounded a corner just ahead; she followed it. She stopped frequently, because the sound was not constant. She would stand still and listen and then continue in the direction of the sound.

She left the path and soon found two small scrawny, twisted acacia trees growing beside a dry gully in the desert floor. Between the trees, a Land Rover was parked.

She approached to within about ten yards of the vehicle and stood motionless. She could faintly see two figures through the windows of the Land Rover. Both figures sat upright. Brittney knew that she had stumbled into a fairly intense makeout session. She began to back away when her shoe scraped against a rock.

Both faces in the Land Rover turned toward her. Brittney ducked quickly, trying to hide among the shadows and the rocks. She stood motionless as the two startled faces in the vehicle peered out into the night. After a few moments, the couple resumed their activity, and Brittney began to steal her way back to the path, having recognized both occupants of the Land Rover: Bryan Rhodes and Susan Arens, the girl he had taken to Mizpeh Ramon.

She found the path back to camp and settled into a brisk pace up the slope. Her thoughts no longer revolved around imagined dangers or suspicious sounds; she thought about Bryan. She couldn't believe it was Bryan in that makeout session in the Land Rover; Susan was way too young for him. It was just too creepy. And how did he get the Land Rover? Susan's mother was one of the archaeologists at Har Karkom, of course, but she certainly wouldn't let Bryan and Susan go joyriding in the desert. *Susan must have gotten access to the keys somehow*, she figured, *but I still can't believe it!*

By the time she arrived at camp, Brittney was sweating lightly from the exertion of her climb up the mountain path in the cool night air. Her calves ached already from her up-hill hike. She stole quietly through the darkened camp and made it to her tent without being discovered.

She opened the tent flap and tiptoed past the empty cot. The light of the full moon illuminated the tent's interior with a dull glow. She stood silently at the foot of Darcelle's cot for a few moments and watched the rhythmic rise and fall of her sleeping form. Finally she stepped past her friend's cot to her own.

She slid between the sheets and reviewed the events of the evening. Jason had been so great when she told him about Matt; she had actually started to believe that Jason was different, and that the things Matt expected of her were unreasonable. But now, after the events at the water hole and stumbling across Bryan and Susan in the Land Rover, maybe she was wrong. Maybe she was naive to expect any boy to love her for who she was instead of for what he could get out of her. Maybe she was being unfair to expect Matt to wait four or five years to experience what other girls would give him right now. Maybe God was unfair to expect that too.

She screwed her eyes shut and wished she could forget about this night, forget about everything.

Jason, Avi, and Philip had long since filed into their tents when Bryan drove Mrs. Arens's Land Rover into camp. He switched off the vehicle's headlights as he entered the moonlit cluster of tents. The tires skidded on the dirt and gravel of the camp road as he jerked to a stop near Susan's tent. He leaned across the space between the two front seats, and met Susan's lips in a prolonged kiss.

She skipped down from the Land Rover and disappeared quickly and quietly into her tent. The Land Rover lurched into motion again as Bryan steered it toward the area at the edge of camp where the vehicles were kept when not in use.

Suddenly, a figure leaped in front of him in the rocky lane. Bryan slammed his foot on the brake and came to a rocking stop just inches from the shadowy form of a soldier. Bryan peered, wide-eyed, through the windshield; the uniformed figure pointed a rifle at him.

"Get out," the man said. "Slowly."

8

Arresting Developments

Har Karkom remained quiet until nearly seven o'clock on Saturday mornings. Though only a few of the dig personnel and volunteers were observant Jews like Shebtai Levitt, the sabbath was honored; no excavation was conducted, and all staff were given the day off.

Volunteers were expected to fend for themselves on the sabbath; no meals were prepared, but the kitchen was open for those who remained in camp. Most of the locals returned home for the sabbath, and many of the volunteers spent Saturdays sightseeing. All, however, were required to return by 9:00 P.M., for the curfew was strictly enforced every night of the week.

Brittney and Darcelle were eating a breakfast of corn flakes and goat's milk (a staple of camp life that Brittney still had not grown accustomed to) when Jason and Philip entered the mess tent. The boys exchanged mumbled greetings with the girls and shuffled sleepily into the kitchen.

Jason and Philip returned to the table and sat across from Darcelle and Brittney. Jason wanted desperately to talk to Brittney about last night and tell her he was sorry; but he didn't know if Brittney had told Darcelle about any of it, and he didn't want to further mess things up between him and Brittney by embarrassing her anymore. Not that he could do any worse than he'd already done, he told himself. He figured whatever hope he might have had of supplanting Matt in Brittney's affection was now completely ruined. He searched Brittney's face for encouragement, and found none. She didn't even look at him.

Suddenly Philip planted his hands on the table and leaned over his food to whisper conspiratorially between Darcelle and Brittney.

"Did you hear about Bryan?" he whispered.

Brittney shifted nervously on the rickety bench. She didn't hide her irritation with Jason and Philip, but Philip's question intrigued her. Did he know about Bryan and Susan? She glanced at Darcelle and then back to the boys. "No," she said haltingly. "What?"

"He was busted last night. I guess one of the guards caught him out past curfew. He was actually driving a Land Rover through camp."

"Was he alone?" Brittney asked quickly.

"Well, yeah," Philip answered. "Why?"

Jason watched the conversation in agony. Brittney still had not talked to him, but had addressed herself only to Philip.

Brittney ignored the question. "What are they going to do to him?" she asked.

Philip shrugged and shoveled a spoonful of cereal into his mouth. "I don't know," he mumbled through the food. "He'll probably just get a demerit. Maybe a couple."

The conversation ceased as Bryan entered the mess tent. He strode into the kitchen without a glance at the group; a moment later he came out with a bowl of cereal and a glass of orange drink. He selected a table at the far corner of the mess tent and positioned himself with his back to the others. Darcelle picked up her breakfast dishes, whispered a few quick words to the others, and walked over to join Bryan at his table.

As soon as Darcelle left the table, Jason leaned across to Brittney.

"Look, about last night—"

Brittney blushed. "Forget it, OK?" She did not look at Jason or Philip.

"No, listen, we didn't really go skinny-dipping."

She lifted her eyes and gave Jason a wary look.

"It was just a joke, that's all," he said. "We were waving our shirts—"

"And Avi was waving her towel," Philip interjected.

"We were just playing around. I wouldn't have let you . . ." He reached across the table and picked up her thin fingers. She did not withdraw her hand. "It was all my idea, and I feel really bad. It was a stupid thing to do."

Brittney and Jason faced each other. She did not break his gaze.

"I'm sorry I messed things up, Brittney," Jason said, after a long moment of silence. He wished he could say more. He wished he could express to her how sorry he was, and why he was sorry . . . because he wanted to mean more to her than just a friend. "I didn't mean to embarrass you or make you mad; I was just being my usual dumb self."

She blushed again, only with a shy smile this time. "It's OK," she said. She dropped her glance. "I shouldn't have been taking a chance like that anyway . . . not with two de-merits against me." She paused. "You guys made it back to your tent last night, right? You didn't get caught, did you?"

"No," Philip answered.

"And we have to make sure we keep quiet about it now," Jason said.

"Especially me," Brittney said. "I've got two demerits, remember? One more and I'm outta here."

"So we just have to keep our mouths shut about last night and everything will be fine. Okay?" Jason looked at Brittney, who nodded seriously, then to Philip.

The sabbath was winding down at Har Karkom when a brown Jeep rumbled into camp, stirring a trail of dust that swirled in the air long after the vehicle had stopped. A curly-haired man in sunglasses emerged from the passenger's side; the Israeli soldier who had driven the Jeep stepped smartly to the man's side as together they walked to the dig director's quarters.

Moments later, they emerged and marched to Philip, Jason, and Bryan's tent. Bryan and Philip were reclining on their cots when the three men entered; Jason sat on the end of Bryan's cot playing his hand-held video game.

"Your batteries are getting low," Jason had just said to Bryan as he bent over his game of Nolo's Revenge. He looked up when the men entered.

"Bryan," Shebtai said. "These men would like to ask you some questions."

Bryan propped himself up on his cot on his elbows. "Why?" he asked. "What's going on?"

"You will please to come with us?" the man in sunglasses said.

Shebtai extended an arm, as if he were halting the other men from proceeding farther into the tent. He exhaled loudly. "There was a disturbance last night in Mizpeh Ramon," he said. "A grocery store owned by an Arab family was—was vandalized. The walls and floor were painted with anti-Arab slogans. The person who did these things was seen leaving the store in one of our Land Rovers."

The three boys exchanged wide-eyed glances.

"So," Bryan said, "what's this have to do with me?"

Doran has informed me that you returned to camp late last night . . . in a Land Rover.

Bryan sat up and swung his legs over the side of the cot. A bright flush of red crept up the back of his neck. "You think I did it?"

The three Israeli men and three American boys faced each other; no one spoke. The soldier stood silently, his rifle slung upright over his shoulder, pointing to the roof of the tent.

Bryan broke the silence with an indignant shout.

"This is crazy!"

"You will come with me," the man in sunglasses said sharply. The soldier shifted his rifle and held it in both hands. The muzzle still pointed upward, but the move was nonetheless threatening.

Shebtai turned and faced the other men. "Just a minute," he said firmly. "There is no reason to—"

"This is a matter of national security," the man answered loudly.

"You cannot march into my camp and arrest one of my volunteers!"

"I didn't do it!" Bryan shouted, but Shebtai and the man were arguing between themselves. "Why can't you people listen to me?" He turned to Philip and Jason. "Tell them I didn't do it!"

Philip and Jason exchanged helpless looks with Bryan. Shebtai and the man in sunglasses were speaking in Hebrew, both of them talking at the same time.

"I can't believe this is happening," Bryan said. "This is crazy! This whole place is insane." He turned to Philip and Jason, as if to defend himself to them. "I didn't do it. All I did was—" He stopped in mid-sentence.

"Wait a minute! I can prove it!" Bryan's expression suddenly brightened. He stood and loudly interrupted the two men. "I can prove it wasn't me."

The three men stared, unsmiling, at Bryan.

He adopted a reasoning, diplomatic tone, but his voice shook as if he were shivering with cold. "I did take a Land Rover out last night, but I didn't go anywhere near that place. I was with a girl." He flashed a quick glance at Jason and Philip. "Susan Arens. All you have to do is ask her."

Shebtai spoke to the curly-haired man in English and explained that Susan's mother was the antiquities expert for the dig. The man nodded. Shebtai and Bryan led the soldier and the man in sunglasses to Susan Arens's tent. Philip and Jason followed.

Shebtai introduced the man in sunglasses to Susan's mother in Hebrew, then explained the situation and related Bryan's claim of having been with her daughter the previous evening. Mrs. Arens called to Susan, who appeared immediately in the door of the tent, as if she had been listening to everything.

Her mother spoke rapidly to Susan in Italian. Bryan and the others watched as fourteen-year-old Susan's eyes grew wide, and she began to answer her mother with a flurry of words and gestures. She had not looked at Bryan once since coming out of the tent; after a few moments, her speech slowed and she finished, crossing her arms against her chest.

Mrs. Arens turned to Shebtai. "Susan says she knows the boy," she said, nodding her head at Bryan. "She says she was in Mizpeh Ramon and that the boy became offended when the, eh, merchants responded to the afternoon call to prayer."

"Is this true?" the man in sunglasses asked Shebtai.

"She says," Mrs. Arens continued, speaking to Shebtai, "that you had to warn him not to make a disturbance."

"Is this true?" the man demanded.

Shebtai sighed. "Yes, that is true." He trained his eyes upon Mrs. Arens. "But you have not said if she was with the boy last night."

Mrs. Arens shot her daughter a hard glance and spoke to her in Italian. Susan's gaze never left her mother's face. She answered in a single syllable that everyone there understood.

"No," she said quietly.

"What!" Bryan protested. "She's lying!" He stepped toward Susan, and Shebtai gripped his arm tightly. "Susan, tell the truth—come on! They're going to arrest me!"

"You will not be arrested," the Israeli official said flatly, turning his sunglasses on Shebtai. He did not look at Bryan. "You will be sent back to your country."

"You can't *do* that," Bryan insisted. "I didn't do it," he repeated, his voice shrinking to a futile whisper.

The crowd fell silent for a few moments, until Shebtai turned to Bryan with pain written on his face. Jason and Philip watched, speechless, breathless, at the unfolding events.

"There is nothing I can do. You will pack your things," Shebtai said, facing Bryan, "and leave early Monday morning."

Bryan held his hands out in front of him, palms up, like a beggar soliciting donations. He grunted several times, as if he was trying to say something, but couldn't quite form what he wanted to say into words. Finally, he managed to speak. "I didn't do it," he said. "I was nowhere near that place last night." He cast a pleading glance at Susan, but she ducked into her tent, followed by her mother.

9

A Multiple Choice Test

Bryan returned to his tent to pack. Jason and Philip dashed to Brittney and Darcelle's tent to inform the girls about what had happened. They stood outside the girls' tent, calling impatiently for them to come out. Darcelle appeared quickly; Brittney emerged a moment after Darcelle, looking as though she had been awakened by their summons.

Darcelle's face clouded with concern as the boys took turns relating the shocking news of the Israeli official's arrival with a soldier at the boys' tent, and the scene that occurred with Susan and her mother. Brittney's face paled in the bright afternoon light, and she covered her mouth with her hand.

"You don't think he did it, do you?" Philip asked, thinly concealing his delight at Bryan's implication.

"No," Darcelle answered quietly. "He wouldn't."

"I agree with Darcelle," Jason said. "I mean, Bryan can be obnoxious, but I don't think he'd do something like that."

"Do you think he was really with that girl?" Philip asked.

"It doesn't much matter, does it?" Jason said. "He was out in a Land Rover after curfew, and if the girl won't vouch for him, he's sunk."

"How did Bryan take it?" Darcelle asked.

"Okay, I guess. He could have done a lot worse." Jason smiled. "He didn't call anybody an unwashed heathen or a godless pagan."

"I'm glad he's going," Philip said bluntly. The others looked at him, surprise registering on their faces. "Well, I'm sorry, but he's starting to really get on my nerves. I mean, he was telling some African dude at the dig yesterday that he was lost and going to hell without Jesus."

"Well, Philip—" Darcelle started, but Philip interrupted her.

"I know what you're going to say, Darcelle: He was witnessing for Jesus." Philip adopted a sarcastic, sugary tone. "It was just embarrassing, that's all. And the African guy definitely did not want to hear it."

"I have to admit, things could be a lot nicer around here with Bryan gone," Jason said.

Brittney turned and ducked into the tent without a word to anyone.

"I can't believe you two!" Darcelle said. "I'm going to look for Shebtai and find out if there's anything we can do about this whole mess."

"That's a good idea," Jason said. "I'll come too." He turned to Philip. "How about you?" Philip shook his head. He flashed a satisfied smile. "I'm going to go help Bryan pack."

Brittney kicked her shoes off and curled into a ball on her cot. She turned her face toward the back wall of the tent and stared at the lines in the faded fabric. The news of Bryan's problem had hit her hard. She was the only person, other than Bryan and Susan, who knew the truth about where Bryan had gone and what he had done last night. But no one knew she knew.

But I can't say anything, she reasoned, *because if I admitted I saw Bryan and Susan in the Land Rover down the mountain, I'd be admitting that I was out past curfew. That would be my third demerit, and I'd be the one going home, not Bryan.*

But those other two demerits were stupid, she objected in defense of herself. *They weren't my fault.*

She closed her eyes and held her head between her hands.

At least it's Bryan, she consoled herself. *I'd be really upset if it was Jason, or even Philip. But Bryan's been such a pain, it's almost like he deserves to go home.* She remembered Bryan's conduct on the plane and in Mizpeh Ramon. *No wonder they think he's the one who did all that stuff to the grocery store.*

She began to replay in her mind the events of the night before: the hike to the water hole with Avi, Philip, and Jason; her embarrassment when she thought they were skinny-dipping; her retreat back up the mountain path toward camp; her discovery of the Land Rover and the faces of Bryan and Susan peering out at her in the moonlight.

In a way, it's his own fault. He shouldn't have been out there with Susan in the first place. She's too young for him; he just wanted to go out with her because he couldn't have Avi.

She pulled her pillow out from under her head and hugged it to her chest. *Besides, if I told anyone what I knew, I wouldn't be the only one in trouble. I'd be telling on Avi and Philip and Jason; they'd all get in trouble too. It would be wrong to rat on my friends.*

She turned over and spun herself into a sitting position on the edge of the cot. *It's not like he's going to jail or anything, Brittney*, she told herself. She cleared her throat as if she were about to speak. *He's just going home. That's not going to break anyone's heart. I might be doing us all a favor—even Bryan. He'd probably end up getting sent home anyway.* "All you have to do," she said aloud, looking around the tent as if to be sure no one could hear her, "is keep your mouth shut and wait for the whole thing to blow over."

She inhaled deeply and let out a long sigh. A voice in her head seemed to assure her, "You're doing the right thing, Brittney Marsh."

She smiled with secret satisfaction.

☆　☆　☆

"Excellent!" Maury, the spectacled demon nerd, scratched his turtle head and snorted his delight. He patted the sophisticated apparatus on the command console in front of him as if it were a purring cat.

Ratsbane's mandibles spread into an obnoxious sneer as he watched his superior work, telling himself that Maury was doing nothing that Ratsbane himself couldn't do as well or better.

"She's buying it," Maury said, cackling gleefully. "She's taking to it like a baby takes a bottle."

Maury suddenly stood from the wheeled chair he had occupied since taking over command of the keyboard from Ratsbane. He swept a turtle hand toward the chair in a grandiose gesture.

"You may return to your station, Demon Ratsbane," Maury announced with a flourish.

Ratsbane shook his head slightly in disgust at his superior's behavior and resisted the urge to slap Maury's glasses off his face. He slid into the chair, positioning his thin frog fingers on the keyboard.

"Not even *you* could mess things up now," Maury said. "I have arranged things with my customary genius and aplomb." He pointed to Brittney Marsh's image on the video screen. "The old guy's menacing stories were really starting to get to her . . . but I've turned things around very nicely, if I do say so myself." He wagged his head with self-satisfaction. "I've got her focusing on what's in her own selfish interest, not on what's right or wrong . . . or even what's best for her in the long run." Maury didn't smile, but his eyes sparkled with pleasure. "She's playing my song," he said.

Ratsbane keyed in a swift command and Brittney's image on the screen blurred, then dissolved into a picture of Darcelle and Jason walking together toward Shebtai and Avi's tent.

"These two are still dangerous," Maury admitted.

"Tell me about it," Ratsbane said, frustration present in his screechy voice. "They've been a *thorn in my side* since the

Westcastle Rebellion." He emitted a sharp, squeaky growl at the images on the screen.

"Okay, my vile assistant—here's the drill," Maury said. "From this moment on, we must keep them all focused on themselves, and then prod them to make their decisions about right and wrong based on their own selfish interests and pleasures." He leaned a scaly hand on the desk and peered at the screen. "Bring up the other two," he instructed Ratsbane, "and let me see what they're up to."

The colors on the screen bled together and coalesced into the figures of Philip and Bryan, who were working together to zip Bryan's bulging suitcase shut.

"These two," Maury said, "have served my purposes well. *Very well.* Neither of them has a clue about how to tell right from wrong. Philip is resisting the Enemy's advances very well, indeed." He waved a hand at the images on the screen as if he were batting at a mosquito. "And Bryan just sees his relationship with the Enemy as a matter of following a lot of dos and don'ts. He's not likely to understand the truth anytime soon."

"Heh-heh," Ratsbane cackled. "Heh-heh-heh."

Maury slapped his assistant's head from behind. "You've been watching cable television again, haven't you?"

The Inside Story:
Commit to God's Way

As if she doesn't have enough to worry about, now Brittney is in another predicament. She can keep her mouth shut and let Bryan take the blame for something he didn't do. Or she can tell the truth, which will clear Bryan but cause trouble for her friends. It will also result in serious consequences for her, since a third demerit will mean she will be sent home.

Given such unattractive choices, Brittney isn't sure which choice is right. Is it right to let Bryan be blamed for something he didn't do? Is it right to get Jason, Philip, and Avi in trouble? How can it be right to turn in your friends? How can it be wrong to simply say nothing?

Once again, however, she's trying to come to a conclusion about which course of action is right and which is wrong on her own—according to her situation, according to what she thinks, according to which choice features the most attractive immediate benefits.

Ratsbane and Maury, of course, are encouraging all that, because they know what could happen if Brittney were to reach a decision based on the concepts Shebtai shared with her. They know that comparing her attitude and actions to God could not only help Brittney determine the right thing to do in her current situation; it could also ruin their long-term plans for her and the others, if she actually commits to God's way.

COMMIT TO GOD'S WAY. Brittney has reasoned that her keeping quiet about Bryan is justified—that it is acceptable to say nothing and allow Bryan to be blamed for the incident in town. A voice in her head assures her, *You're doing the right thing, Brittney Marsh.*

But is it right for her to remain silent—is it wrong for her not to tell? Instead of comparing her attitude or action to God and what He says to answer that question, she is determining it is right to keep quiet based on her own subjective view. And based on *her view,* it does seem right to keep silent.

It will be impossible for Brittney to commit to God's way on this matter as long as she continues to look to herself for moral guidance. She is not seeing objectively. She has her selfish interest at heart and that selfish interest "blinds" her to the absolute truth.

To commit to God's way, Brittney must turn from her selfishness and look to God as her standard. She can do this by first asking: "What precepts or commands of God relate to my situation?"

In the course of God's revelation to Moses on Mount Sinai, He gave us some very specific commands:

Do not steal.

Do not lie.

Do not deceive one another.

Do not swear falsely . . .

Do not defraud your neighbor or rob him (see Lev. 19:11-13).

God made it abundantly clear to His people, to you and to me, and to Brittney—by precept —that deceit is wrong.

God's negative commands against deceit reflect a positive principle. This principle serves, like an umbrella, to protect all who stay within its boundaries.

That principle, of course, is honesty—the quality of being truthful, transparent, and trustworthy. In many ways, honesty is defined by what it will not do.

Honesty will not cheat. "Do not be deceived," Paul warned, ". . . swindlers will [not] inherit the kingdom of God" (1 Cor. 6:10).

Honesty will not steal. It is the honest person's goal "not to steal . . . but to show that [he] can be fully trusted" (Titus 2:10).

Honesty will not lie. "Therefore," the Bible says, "each of you must put off falsehood and speak truthfully to his neighbor" (Eph. 4:25).

Brittney reasons that not saying anything about Bryan can't be wrong. And, of course, one can't find a Scripture passage that states, "Thou shalt not keep silent about Bryan." But the principle of honesty requires transparency and integrity. If she compares her action to God's principle of honesty, Brittney will understand that her silence hides the truth and is, in fact, a form of deceit.

But the principle of honesty does not possess intrinsic value; it is a virtue because it springs from the nature and character of God Himself.

Honesty is right (and dishonesty wrong) because God is true. Truth is not something God does, nor is it something He possesses; it is a part of who He is.

In the wilderness of Horeb, Moses sang, "He is the Rock, his work is perfect . . . a God of truth and without iniquity, just and right is he" (Deut. 32:4 KJV).

God is true and there is nothing false in Him. It is His nature, therefore, that defines honesty as moral, and dishonesty, fraud, and deceit as evil.

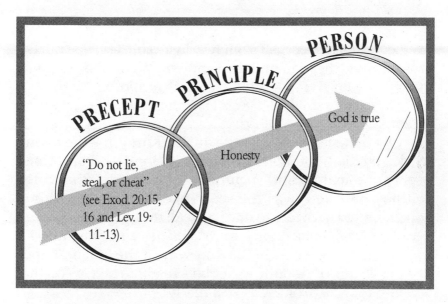

If Brittney can see God as He is, a God who is true by His very nature, she will see that deceit is wrong and honesty is right in her situation. Honesty is right, not because there is a law that says "tell what you know," but because a God of truth requires transparency and integrity—**for all people, for all times, and for all places.**

10

A Mountaintop Experience

Brittney extracted a brush from her dusty suitcase. She ran the brush through her hair and then gathered all the loose strands into a pony tail, tying it into place with a colored band.

Sure will be good to take a shower tomorrow, she thought. *At last.*

Of all the hardships of life at Har Karkom—the taxing work, the heat, the tents, the dust, the meals (comprised mostly of tomatoes and cucumbers, it seemed)—the worst, Brittney reflected, was the scarcity of water for bathing, which limited showers to once a week for those who stayed in camp. *I don't think my hair's ever been this dirty,* she figured.

Darcelle appeared in the doorway of the tent and nodded her head to the south. "Shebtai's ready to take us on that walking tour he promised. You ready?"

Brittney nodded. "Sure," she said. She tossed the brush onto the suitcase and reached for her shoes. She automatically turned the shoes upside down and shook them, a habit she developed in the last couple days after hearing tales of the scorpions populating the area that often concealed themselves in shoes.

"Is Shebtai going to do anything about Bryan?" Brittney asked as she tied her shoes and stood to her feet.

Darcelle's expression clouded. She shook her head. "He said if Bryan couldn't account for where he was last night, there's nothing he can do about it."

Brittney lowered her gaze to the floor of the tent. "That's too bad."

"Yeah," Darcelle said. "I tried to get Bryan to come with us, but he wouldn't. He's pretty upset."

Brittney and Darcelle met Jason and Philip at the mess tent; Shebtai and Avi arrived moments later. The six of them discussed Bryan's predicament in funeral tones and expressions until Darcelle faced Shebtai and said, "If we're going to finish before dark, shouldn't we get started?"

Shebtai smiled. "Oh, you do not have to worry about that." He lifted his gaze to the sky, clapped his hands together once, and summoned everyone to follow him.

Darcelle fell into step beside Shebtai. Jason and Brittney walked together, and Philip deftly clasped Avi's hand in his and trailed slightly behind the others.

"You have already learned much about the treasures of Har Karkom," Shebtai said as they hiked toward the summit of the loaf-shaped mountain. "You have seen the religious rock art, some of it four or five thousand years old, that testifies to the fact that this place was considered sacred for many, many years."

"This," he continued, pointing to a crude stone pillar set on end, like the one Avi had pointed out to Brittney the night before, "is called a *menhir*." He pronounced the word quickly, almost rhyming it with "veneer." They approached the stone monolith, and Shebtai stood beside it as he continued his narration.

"It probably marked a stopping point for worshipers ascending toward the mount, perhaps like the stations on the *Via Dolorosa*—the way of the cross. Since it appears to be the last *menhir* on the way to the top of the mount, this stone may have marked a boundary, a line that ordinary worshipers were not allowed to cross."

He crossed his right arm against his chest, and rested his left elbow on that arm. He propped his index finger against his lips and nose, and left it there as he spoke. "In the Scriptures," he said, a glint in his eyes and a quiet intensity that made his voice sound a full octave lower, "when the children of Israel gathered at Mount Sinai, God instructed Moses to put limits around the mountain so the people would not trespass on the holy mountain. Do you remember?"

No one answered; they stared at Shebtai with intense interest.

He shrugged. "This stone may have marked that kind of boundary." He turned and resumed his walk up the steep incline. A determined look etched deep lines into his face as he walked, as if he were searching for something or someone.

As they continued their journey up Har Karkom, only Shebtai spoke; an air of mystery seemed to surround them and echo their every step through the vast brown plains of the southern Negev below. Finally, Shebtai stopped at the crest and stared out at the vast expanse of dirt and rock below. The setting sun painted the western sky with a palette of purple and scarlet; the barren peaks of the central Negev, their outline thrown into sharp contrast by the low light of the dying day, rose on the other side of the group.

Brittney, Darcelle, Jason, Philip, and Avi clustered around their guide and traced his gaze. He finally inhaled deeply, as if he was sorry to break the silence and stillness. He pointed to a location on the desert floor below; the shade of the ground around that point differed from the dirt all around, giving evidence that it had been excavated.

"That is Site Number 52," he said. "It was excavated over ten years ago."

The group of teenagers squinted at the unremarkable assortment of rocks a short distance from the base of the mountain on which they stood.

"It is hard to see from this height," Shebtai said, "but if you look closely you will identify a design: twelve standing stones grouped together beside the remains of a structure."

Darcelle and Jason nodded; Philip muttered, "Uh-huh."
"That structure was not a home; it contained a platform
and a courtyard, and we do not think it was roofed." He
paused significantly. "It was probably an altar of some sort."
"Like a tabernacle?" Darcelle asked.
"The Scriptures say that after Moses received the Law
from God on Mount Sinai, he built an altar at the foot of
the mountain and erected twelve sacred pillars to repre-
sent the twelve tribes of Israel."
"That was the tabernacle?" Darcelle's voice had risen in
pitch.
Shebtai shook his head. "Perhaps the predecessor to the
tabernacle." He gazed intently at the group. Red-haired Avi
smiled back at him as if she and her father shared a secret.
"Immediately after he built the altar and the twelve stones,
Moses returned to the mountain and received instructions
from God for the construction of the tabernacle."
"Are you saying—" Jason began. He stopped in
mid-sentence, turning from Site Number 52, where his gaze
had been riveted, to look directly at Shebtai Levitt. "Are you
saying this is Mount Sinai?"
Shebtai returned Jason's gaze steadily, without changing expression. "Let me show you something else," he said.
"Step this way."
Shebtai led them across the rocky summit of the mountain. The western sky had changed colors to a dull mixture
of gray and brown. He stopped at an array of stones on the
eastern side of Har Karkom.
Philip, Brittney, Jason, and Darcelle each recognized the
excavated outline of a small temple, with an elevated platform in the midst of a courtyard, much like Site Number 52,
only these ruins were at nearly the highest point on the
mountain.
"When God directed Moses in designing the tabernacle,
He repeatedly used the phrase, 'As you were shown on the
mountain.' Many people think God may have shown Moses

a vision of the completed tabernacle, or perhaps even etched the plans into rock. It is also possible that God showed Moses an actual, physical model . . . on the mountain."

"This is *too much*," Jason whispered reverently.

Without a word, Shebtai sprang into motion and climbed quickly to a point, not fifty feet from the temple ruins, that was slightly higher than anything else around it. As the group approached, what had earlier looked like a mound of rocks was seen to be a solid outcropping of rock with an angular cavity just about the size and height of a one-man tent.

"Wow," Brittney said, her voice barely audible.

Shebtai's eyes blazed; his gray-and-black eyebrows formed twin tents over his eyes, casting them into shadows that were broken only by the sparks of light that seemed to rise from deep within Shebtai's soul. "When Moses asked to see God's glory," he said, "God explained, 'You cannot see my face, for no mortal can see me and live. But there is a place beside me. Stand on the rock, and when my glory passes by, I will place you in the cleft of the rock, and will cover you with my hand until I have passed by. Then I will take away my hand and you will see my back, but my face must not be seen.'"

"I have been on many mountains in this land," Shebtai continued, "but I have never seen a formation like this."

"This is *really* Mount Sinai?" Philip asked. "Where Moses got the Ten Commandments?"

"If this is the mountain of God, it is the holiest site imaginable to a Jew, because the Law—more than the land of Israel, more than the Temple, more than anything else—the Law is what made us a people. It was in the Law that the God of Israel revealed Himself, expressed Himself, to all people, because the Law proceeds from His nature."

Shebtai's eyes sparkled with passion. He looked from Darcelle to Brittney, and then from Jason to Philip. "Do you understand what that means? Not just to an ancient tribe, but to us today?" His question met only interested looks from the group. He drew a slow breath.

"When you go to a doctor, what do you expect him to do?" Jason spoke first. "Tell me what's wrong with me."

"And maybe write a prescription to cure it," Darcelle added.

Shebtai smiled. "That is exactly what God did," he said, clapping his hands together and speaking loudly, animatedly. "The Law is God's prescription for us! It tells us what is wrong with us, and what is right with us . . . and it does it by showing us what He is like. The Law teaches us that truthfulness is right, because it is like God Himself; He is true. The Law teaches us that purity is a good thing, because He is pure. The Law teaches us that what is like God—the God of Torah, the God who revealed Himself in the Law--is right, and what is not like Him is wrong." He gazed at the rocky summit of the mount, and his eyes glistened with tears. "To have been part of that great company who first received the Law from God Himself—what an honor that would have been."

The group fell silent again. The group on the mountain stood as still and silent as the stone *menhirs* that guarded the mountain. Their every sense, their very souls, seemed alive to the special place to which Shebtai had led them. All of them, even Philip, felt as if they were standing on holy ground.

A wind suddenly stirred the dust on the hill around them. Shebtai finally broke the silence. He smiled and lifted a face to the sky. "We can remain for fifteen minutes if you wish to have some time for . . . for thinking, or praying. If you wish."

☆　☆　☆

"How did this happen?" Maury's green turtle-face reddened dangerously. "I turn my back for a moment and you've got that old guy carrying on again about how the Law reveals the Enemy as the standard for right and wrong! What's *wrong* with you?"

Ratsbane typed furiously at the keyboard as Maury ranted and raved. He continued typing as he defended himself against Maury's vile stream of accusations. "I was concentrating on 9745," he explained, bringing up a picture of Bryan onto the screen. "When I checked back on some of the others, they were already on the mountain talking about *Moses*—he spat onto the floor of the laboratory—and the giving of the Law." He spat again, twice.

"Didn't you *do* anything?" Maury protested.

"Of course, I did," Ratsbane answered, still typing furiously. "But none of it's working," he grumbled in a squeaky voice.

Maury growled with frustration. "That's because you're still toying with temptation, trying to get them to do *this* wrong thing or *that* wrong thing," he said. *"You're* playing chopsticks!" he shouted, straightening himself and raising his arms like a conductor preparing to lead an orchestra. But *I* am performing a concerto!"

He shouldered Ratsbane off the keyboard and began tapping and typing with apparent ease, chattering like an auctioneer as he worked. "Even if they've been exposed to the truth, even if they are beginning to understand that the Enemy is the Source of truth, even if they discover how to tell right from wrong, we've still got a few tricks in the bag."

"But," Ratsbane interjected, "if they look to the Enemy's nature and character as their Source of truth, their Powerlink with Him will be reinforced; they'll be drawing power from the very Spirit of the Enemy Himself!"

"Yes, ant-face," Maury agreed, still working the keyboard like a concert pianist. "But if we can distract them and deter them from the right choices, we can disrupt the Powerlink! Because even after they discover the truth, they still must *commit to* the truth! And that's where we can still make marvelous music!"

"All right, maestro," Ratsbane sneered. "So what do we do?"

"First," he said, speaking in a steady monotone as if speaking to himself, "I fire off an E-mail message to Natural Disaster Subsector 6491 and have them whip up a sudden desert storm."

Ratsbane's mutant mouth emitted a surprised screech. He begrudgingly had to admit he was impressed. "You can do *that?*"

"That will help me," Maury continued, ignoring his assistant, "to distract them from all that prattle about the Law and the Sovereign Lord of the Universe. With any luck, I can use fear to erase most of what the old guy said."

Ratsbane's eyes suddenly sparkled, and his mandibles spread open in a grotesque grin. "What did you call Him?"

"Who?"

"The Enemy."

"I called Him—" Maury suddenly realized his mistake. He had referred to the Enemy by using names that are forbidden, names that may not be uttered by a demon of Hell. "Don't distract me, scissorlips," he growled. "I've got a lot of work ahead of me if I'm going to undo the damage *you've* caused."

He turned his face to the console and began typing nervously. He watched Ratsbane's smiling visage from the corners of his eyes as he stroked a few more keys; the video image of the group on the mountain was suddenly surrounded with a frame of cryptic meters and gauges, indicating red and blue lines of varying lengths and widths.

"Next, I get 8744," he continued, pointing to Brittney's image on the screen, "to focus on the immediate benefits of making the wrong choice . . . and the unpleasant consequences of the right choice."

"What are you talking about?" Ratsbane croaked. "The dumbest demon in hell knows there's no benefit to making wrong choices!"

"*Immediate* benefits, toad-brain," Maury snapped. "I said *immediate* benefits!"

The Inside Story: Count on God's Protection and Provision

A fast-food restaurant chain advertises their hamburgers with the promise that you can have it your way, right away.

They're not dumb; they know that slogan will appeal to a lot of people, because most of us want our own way, and we want it now!

Maury knows that too. He knows that even when human beings learn to measure right and wrong according to God's nature and character, it doesn't guarantee that they will *choose* right. The battle isn't over when they *discern* what's right; they must still *do* what's right by committing to God's way. But Maury knows that many wrong choices offer immediate "benefits," while right choices often seem to hold more long-range results. Sin is often packaged very appealingly and carries a promise of instant gratification. Right choices, on the other hand, often require postponing immediate satisfaction for better long-term results.

Brittney struggled with this issue in her relationship with Matt. In addition to the physical pressures brought about by raging hormones, she felt a deep emotional need to be loved, to feel wanted by a man. As her relationship with Matt became more intense, she was faced with a choice: to enjoy the intensity of sex (which promised immediate gratification) or to save sex for the intimacy of marriage (which offered benefits far greater, though not immediate).

Brittney is only now beginning to realize that the benefits of the wrong choice are as fleeting and unsatisfying as they are immediate.

Brittney faces a similar choice because of what she knows about Bryan. If she chooses to keep her mouth shut, he will be sent home and she will be allowed to stay. If she chooses to reveal what she knows, Bryan will be cleared, but she will get her third demerit and will be the one who is forced to return home. The first choice, obviously, offers Brittney immediate benefits. The second choice is less attractive in the short run, but it holds greater long-term benefits.

The business of hell, of course, is to focus Brittney's attention—and ours—on selfish interests and instant gratification in order to justify wrong choices. In so doing, hell's demons can prevent us from fully learning and experiencing the overwhelming benefits of right choices.

COUNT ON GOD'S PROTECTION AND PROVISION

Remember, God gave us His commands for our own good (see Deut. 10:12-13)—they come out of God's loving motivation to protect us and to provide for us, for the long term. The more Brittney—and you and I—trust in God's loving motivation, the more we will want to commit to His ways. God's standard for honesty, for example, protects and provides for us in so many ways.

God's standard of honesty protects us from guilt and provides a clear conscience. The dishonest person must be always looking over his shoulder, but the young man or woman who heeds God's standard of honesty knows the benefit of "clean hands and a pure heart" (Ps. 24:4).

God's standard of honesty protects us from shame and provides a sense of accomplishment. Anyone who has ever been exposed for lying or cheating knows the embarrassment and shame that is often the price of dishonesty. Such people cheat themselves—of the sense of accomplishment that comes from a good grade, a deserved promotion, or a hard-earned victory.

God's standard of honesty protects us from a cycle of deceit and provides for a reputation of integrity. Lies are like that popular brand of potato chips with the slogan, "Bet you can't eat just one. . . . ;" it's nearly impossible to stop after just one. Lies breed more lies, and deceit leads to more deceit. But a person who habitually tells the truth, even when it may cost him or her, earns a reputation for integrity that "is better than silver or gold" (Prov. 22:1).

God's standard of honesty protects us from ruined relationships and provides for trusting relationships. A fifteen-year-old girl once said to me, "I'll never trust my mother again." I asked her why. "I asked my mom two years ago if she and Dad had waited until marriage to have sex, and she said, yes, they had waited. The other day I found her diary and read it, and I found out she didn't wait. I found out she lied to me." Such broken relationships often result from dishonesty. The element of trust is indispensable in relationships. A strong foundation of trust will improve and enrich the quality of all your relationships, providing something that money can't buy, and dishonesty can't achieve.

Ratsbane and Maury don't want Brittney to see any of those protections and provisions, because they are so overwhelmingly persuasive. They provide solid reasons to say no to her selfish interests and say yes to God's loving commands. The enemy will also work hard at keeping her from understanding God's standards for sexual behavior as well.

God's standard for sexual behavior protects from guilt and provides for spiritual reward. When we transgress God's standards of right and wrong, we invariably suffer guilt. And there are many blessings in a clear conscience, whether that comes through obedience or receiving forgiveness when we transgress.

God's standard for sexual behavior protects from unplanned pregnancy and provides for a healthy atmosphere of child-rearing. Every day in America, 2,795 teenage girls get pregnant and 1,106 have abortions. There are overwhelming pressures on a teenage single mother, not to speak of the difficulty of nurturing a newborn child without the love of a father. The best atmosphere for a child is where they can experience a home where a man and a woman love each other exclusively and are committed to each other for a lifetime.

God's standard for sexual behavior protects from STDs and provides for peace of mind. Every day in America 4,219 teenagers contract a sexually transmitted disease—many of them incurable by modern medicine. That is a scary thought. But one can still have peace of mind, because not one of those diseases have been passed between two mutually faithful partners who entered the relationship sexually pure. Why? Because God's standard for sexual behavior protects from STDs.

God's standard for sexual behavior protects from sexual insecurity and provides for trust. Premarital sexual activity can be a powerfully negative source of insecurity and mistrust in a marriage. "If he couldn't control himself before marriage," the wife reasons, "what makes me think he will control himself in marriage?" "She 'played around' before she met me," the husband figures, "what's to stop her from playing around now?" Sexual purity and faithfulness, on the other hand, provide a sense of security and an atmosphere of trust.

God's standard of sexual behavior protects from emotional distress and provides for true intimacy. The intensity of sex is too often confused with the intimacy of love. A true love that is committed to provide and protect each other, along with purity and faithfulness, is designed to result in an incredible intimate, close, and bonded relationship. Sex is like dynamite; it can either blow a relationship apart or (if it is used as God directed) open up new depths of intimacy, unity, and trust.

When God says no, He does so because He wants to provide for us and to protect us. Brittney Marsh is having trouble seeing that, of course, and that's just what Ratsbane and Maury want. They plan to keep her—and all of us—from seeing the person of God behind the truth, because that is who they fear the most.

11

Sudden Thunder

The group had responded to Shebtai's offer of a brief time of meditation on the mountain by seeking private places where they could be alone with their thoughts. Brittney stumbled slightly as she descended the slope leading away from the cleft, the stone shelter at the highest point in the mountain. She regained her footing and gingerly picked her way down the winding, rocky path. She wanted to spend some time alone at the very edge of the mountain, the craggy ledge that overlooked Site Number 52.

Darcelle had claimed a seat near the cleft, and Philip and Avi had walked slowly back down the trail toward camp. They were silent as they walked, and Philip's thoughts were not for Avi; he was thinking of his father, and the problems between them that had brought him here. He and Avi held hands, but she allowed him the privacy of his own thoughts.

He envied Avi's relationship with her father. He had watched them together, had noticed the way she responded to him, and he to her. He noticed that she related to Shebtai in an entirely different way than he related to his dad. She didn't act like her father was trying to hurt her or anger her with his rules. He wondered if that was because Shebtai was different from his father . . . or because Avi was different from himself. Maybe both.

Jason had stood indecisively beside Shebtai as the group fanned out on the mountain. He watched Brittney as she turned to go away from the group, seeking her own private place. He had hoped to spend these few quiet moments alone with her, but she had acted as if he didn't exist. He was convinced that she was still mad about the incident at the water hole; she had seemed distant all afternoon, and he wished there were some way he could regain her confidence.

Jason dropped his gaze to the ground after Brittney rounded a rocky corner and disappeared from his view. When he looked up again, he met Shebtai's eyes.

The dig director smiled. "She is a lovely young woman," he said.

Jason screwed his face up in an expression of hopelessness.

"But she does not know how you feel," Shebtai said. Jason felt the heat of Shebtai's intense gaze upon him.

Jason shrugged and looked at the ground. He was certain Shebtai could never understand how Jason felt, how he was paralyzed between his fear of rejection and his desperate need for acceptance.

"What do you think she would say if you were honest with her?" Shebtai asked.

"I don't know," Jason answered. He paused long. "She'd probably say we should just be friends."

"And that would be different from the way things are now?"

Jason looked at Shebtai. The man's smile was gone, but the corners of his eyes crinkled with kindness.

Brittney felt her foot twist beneath her as a loose pebble scooted from under her shoe. She threw her weight backward and slid to her seat on the ledge. The pebble bounced over the edge of the precipice that overlooked the sprawling desert plain below. Her heart thumped rapidly, and she reminded herself to be more careful.

She stood slowly and brushed the seat of her pants and leaned her back against the mountain's wall. She gazed over

the edge of the summit, where Shebtai had pointed to the
site of the ancient altar, and the twelve standing stones
beside it. She remembered his words. What must it have
been like to have been there when the Law was given for
the first time, to suddenly have God come down from
heaven and reveal—boom!—what's right and what's
wrong?

A steady wind tousled her brown hair and blew it
across her face as she peered at the expanse of land below. She lifted her hand to her face and held her hair flat
against the side of her head. She imagined a sea of tents
filling that plain, for miles to the south. She glanced to
the west and imagined still more tents and campfires and
goat pens, as the Israelites awaited Moses' return from the
mountain. She imagined the people pausing in their work and
worship to glance at the mountain when they heard a rumble
of thunder on the distant peak. *Is that the voice of God?* they
may have asked. *Is His throne on that summit, or does He dwell
in the clouds that encircle the peak?* Her mouth hung open as she
absorbed the mystery and power of this spot Shebtai called a
special place.

As she turned her gaze to Har Karkom's western valley,
her contemplation was immediately interrupted. Her eyes
widened and she inhaled sharply.

It seemed to her that the sky had suddenly dropped;
dark clouds loomed at the edge of the mountain in the gray
twilight of the dying day. She could not see the peaks of the
Central Negev that she knew were there, nor even the wide
plains of the valley below. The clouds seemed close enough
to touch, and they seemed to be drifting closer every second.

Suddenly she screamed out loud. A flash of white
light pierced the blackness like a bayonet thrust, and a
deafening crack seemed to shake the very ground beneath
her. The clouds were all around her now, the wind increased, and she forgot all about her fantasy of a few
moments ago.

She covered her head with her arms. The wind seemed ready to whip her off the mountain, and she backed away from the dangerous edge of the path. The wind pinned her against the wall of rock that lined the path, and she squinted her eyes against the whirling dust and terrible force of the storm.

She felt panic lodge in her chest and throat like a knife, and she turned to make her way back. She ducked into the wind and fought to climb the path she had come down just moments ago, but the fog shrouded the path and she feared that she would not be able to find her way, and might even plunge to her death off the steep side of the mountain. And, she thought in a panic, she had never been so close to thunder and lightning; she feared the next lightning flash would find her.

She had taken only a step when she put her foot down against the side of a rock, twisting her ankle and flinging her into the dirt and stones in front of her. She broke her fall with her hands and knees, and felt an instant flare of pain. She turned her palms over as she climbed back to her feet, and saw a dull, dark mixture of dirt and blood on the palms of her hands. Her knees burned, and she was sure they were bleeding, too, but she did not pause to inspect them. She was nervously panting now; her eyes flashed and her nostrils flared like a spooked horse.

Light flashed ahead of her, illuminating nothing but the fog all around her, and another clap of thunder prompted a choking scream from her throat. She scrambled to her feet and shuffled to her former position against the rock wall, when a deafening sound behind her, like the beating blades of a helicopter, seemed to bounce off the mountain walls all around her.

As she moved toward the sound a blinding light pierced the fog and surrounded her. She clung to the unmoving mountain wall, afraid to move, afraid to be still, afraid to open her eyes, and afraid to close them. She extended her arms toward the light, trying to peer beyond it to its source, but she could not.

Where is the light coming from, she wondered, frantically looking for its source. Suddenly the light took on a bright fluorescent glow of yellow, then green, then blue, then disappeared as quickly as it had come. It seemed to whirl away, up into the sky, the way smoke from a campfire disappears among the limbs of trees. The deafening sound stopped. The wind ceased. She felt a cold chill sweep over her as if she were being immersed slowly into an icy river.

She opened her mouth to scream, but nothing came out. A paralyzing fear immobilized her as if frozen to the mountain wall. *Oh God, am I dying?* she wondered. As quickly as the wind and sound of the storm had ceased, it returned. Her heart began to beat wildly as the wind again whipped savagely through her shirt, tearing at her hair.

The storm had hit without warning, but Shebtai had sensed something just moments before the dark clouds enveloped the mountain. He and Jason had called to the others and managed to gather them quickly, before the wind and fog would have completely separated them from each other.

Shebtai herded them into a narrow passage where a dry stream bed had cut a shallow crevice in the rock. He instructed them to crouch in the crowded space; they would wait there for the storm to pass.

"Brittney's not here!" Jason shouted frantically at Shebtai, as if it were his fault.

"I know," he answered.

"We can't leave her out there!" Jason's eyes were wide and bright, even in the darkness of the storm. He stood. "We've gotta go find her!"

"You stay here!" Shebtai barked. "I will go."

The darkness now wrapped itself around Brittney like a cloak, dispelled only by frequent flashes of lightning that preceded the thunderous booms that shook the mountain; she found herself now praying aloud, "Oh, God, help me! Please help me!" Her lip quivering and her eyes clouding, she felt overwhelmingly tired as if all her strength had been suddenly drained from her. She considered simply sitting or lying down on the ground and hoping someone would find her.

She felt something graze her cheek. She lifted a hand to her face, and felt a drop of moisture. She felt another, then more. It was raining.

The palms of her hands now throbbed with pain. She tried to inspect her injuries, but the darkness was too thick. She knew the skin must be torn from them. She felt tears welling up in her eyes and throat, but she squelched them. With a grunting cry of determination, she dropped to her hands and knees, and began gingerly crawling through the darkness, telling herself that she could make the trip safely on her hands and knees, with less fear of a misstep that would send her plummeting off the side of the craggy mountain; she could feel her way back up the path toward the rest of the group.

She crawled slowly, carefully, painfully, up the path, praying as she went. Droplets of rain spattered on her and around her; she ignored them. After what seemed hours, she finally dragged herself up a slight incline and spied the tent-like outcropping of rock Shebtai had pointed out to the group. She clawed and clambered her way to the low shelter. She started headfirst into the opening but, deciding she could never turn around inside the small space, turned around and backed in feet-first.

The storm raged outside in the darkness, and even in the shelter of the rock, she shivered with fear. Every flash of lightning and crash of thunder startled her, causing her to jump so much that she once thumped her head against the rocky roof of her haven.

"Make it stop, God," she shouted. "Make it stop!" She cried now, the tears that had long welled in her eyes streaming out.

"You can do anything, God! You can stop the storm right now!" A flash of light and clap of thunder seemed to mock her prayer. The earth seemed to quake and roll beneath her prostrate form, and she feared that her rock shelter would collapse on top of her. She didn't know whether to squeeze herself further into the cramped space or try to escape it, but she felt frozen to the spot, unable to do either.

Is this how Moses met God up here? In a storm? She found herself scared by the thought of God being on that mountain, perhaps in the storm, in a way that He was not present everywhere else. "I don't want to meet You this way, God, because I'm not . . . I'm not . . . I have things I should do. Things I should make right."

Suddenly the darkness deepened until it seemed palpable, as thick and black as used motor oil. She shrunk back into her refuge and began to talk to God as she had never talked to Him before.

"O God," she said. She whispered the phrase over several times, as if it was useless to try to express all that she was thinking and feeling. "O God," she repeated. Her lips formed the words without making a sound. "I know You're more powerful than anything. You can shake this mountain like a little baby's rattle. You could flatten it out like a pancake if You wanted to. You're the most powerful thing there is . . . You're holy, and You're true. You're all those things that Shebtai said, and I . . . I've been so stupid, and so . . . so wrong about so many things."

She continued praying as the wind dwindled and died. An eerie silence covered the mount. Long minutes had passed.

She was perspiring and shaking, but no longer from fear. She was trembling with the realization that something unbelievable had happened to her, not just because of the storm and the light and everything else, but because of what she felt happening inside her. She felt as if she'd been trying to focus a camera in the fog, but now the fog had lifted, and everything seemed much clearer. She now saw very clearly how wrong she had been—and why.

☆   ☆   ☆

A blood-curdling scream echoed in the laboratory of RAID, where Maury and Ratsbane stood shoulder to shoulder frantically working the controls of the great command center.

"Nooooo!" Maury cried repeatedly. "Nooooo! This can't be happening!" He pounded keys and twirled knobs with frenzied intensity.

"It's happening, all right," Ratsbane added as he, too, worked the instruments. The lights on the console flashed rapidly, most of them registering in the dangerous red zone. Some warning lights had apparently burnt out; they flickered weakly, and a few were completely dark.

"No, I'm not finished with her yet," Maury vowed. His turtle claws clicked and clacked against the vast keyboard in rapid rhythm. He recited the litany of his strategies aloud as he worked. "You're almost sixteen now," he chanted, "you're not a little girl anymore. You're old enough to decide things for yourself. Don't let Him tell you what to do. If you cave in to the Enemy, you'll never have any more fun as long as you live! Think of what you'll have to do . . . think of what it'll cost you . . . think of the consequences!"

Ratsbane had stopped pounding the keyboard. He straightened his frog back and stared with his bulbous black eyes at the huge video screen that dominated the RAID lab.

"What are you doing?" Maury snapped at his assistant. "Open the veritractors to full power!"

Ratsbane didn't respond. He continued staring numbly at the screen as if hypnotized.

"Didn't you hear me? I need more power!" Maury screamed, still clacking away at the keyboard.

"It's too late," Ratsbane murmured.

Maury spun his head and looked hatefully at his motionless assistant. He perceived the direction of Ratsbane's gaze. He followed it, turning his own gaze upon the screen.

Above the prostrate form of Brittney Marsh lying in the shelter of the rock, a faint blue-white mist seemed to spiral in the air. As he watched, the mist seemed to float into two distinct shapes.

"What *is* that?" Maury asked, his voice raspy and quiet.

"Brigadiers," Ratsbane answered. "They're brigadiers—angel warriors. They are dancing the *victory dance!*"

"It's too late, Maury," Ratsbane said in a dull, emotionless voice. "It's too late for us. She's yielding to the Enemy. And He is infusing her with His presence . . . and power. It's over."

Maury watched in horror as the vapors congealed into two massive, angelic forms in shining blue-and-white uniforms dancing and shimmering in the air above the rocky shelter where Brittney lay.

☆　☆　☆

Brittney lifted her head and wiped tears of emotion from her eyes. She crawled out of her cramped quarters and stood to her feet, brushing herself off as she stood. The mount appeared unaffected by the storm; the moon shone in a clear sky, with faint wisps of clouds floating far from the height where Brittney stood.

She heard Shebtai's voice, calling her name. He ran to her and folded his big arms around her. She buried her face into her chest and all the emotion of the past hour poured out like a flood.

She heard other voices then, and she turned to see Jason running toward her. She threw her arms around him, and the others crowded around.

"Are you all right, girl?" Darcelle asked.

"Where were you?" Philip asked.

Brittney wiped tears of relief from her eyes and related her experience. She told how she had been trapped on the mountain ledge overlooking Site Number 52, how the noise had approached and the light appeared through the fog, how she had crawled to the shelter and waited out the storm there. They asked her questions, especially about the mysterious light, and she answered them as well as she could, but she finally shrugged her shoulders.

"Look, guys, I can't explain it. I don't know what it was—"

"It was probably a helicopter," Philip said. "Right, Shebtai?"

The man shrugged. "If a helicopter was flying in that storm, its pilot was in greater danger than any of us."

"Sheet lightning!" Jason offered with a snap of his fingers. "Think it could've been that?"

"I don't know, Jason—it may have been," Brittney answered. "But I do know one thing: God was up here with me, and I realized some things during that storm—things that I should have seen a long time ago."

Brittney's face beamed and Jason thought how beautiful she looked and how frightened he was for her when she was on the mountain. "We should be getting back to camp," Shebtai interrupted. "I will lead the way." He smiled at Brittney. "Everyone stay close together this time."

As the group returned to camp, Jason gripped Brittney by the arm and pulled her aside. "I need to talk to you," he said.

"We have to stay with the others," she warned.

"I know, but I have to say something."

She tossed her hair out of her face and listened. Jason continued as they walked side by side, lagging behind the others on the path.

He drew a deep breath and blew it out slowly. "But I've never been able . . . I've always been kind of afraid to, you know, to tell people how I feel, to open up to people, you know? Especially to girls." His chest heaved with a frustrated sigh, as if he was in physical pain.

Brittney read the agony in his face. She reached out and touched his arm. "It's OK, Jason—really it's OK. I want to know how you feel," she said softly. Their eyes met, and he relaxed slightly.

He continued speaking then, breathing unevenly, like a sprinter trying to talk after a short race. "I've just never felt like people would accept me for me," he said. "Even my parents. I mean, they love me, I guess, but it's not like they really go out of their way to listen to me or anything like that. As long as I stay out of trouble and stay out of their way, we get along OK, you know?"

The others had disappeared now, and Jason and Brittney faced each other on the mountain path not far from camp. "This must sound really dumb, huh?" he said.

She had not moved her hand from his arm. "It doesn't sound dumb at all, Jason. Don't stop."

"Well, see, I guess that's why I've always been afraid to really open up to anybody or be honest about how I feel, because I'm afraid if I'm not always joking around or playing games, people won't have time for me—they won't want to spend time with me. But I realized up there," he said, nodding up the mountain path, "that some things are just too important. So I've decided to be honest with you and whatever happens, happens."

Brittney smiled and squeezed Jason's arm slightly. Jason went on then, like a truck picking up speed on a downhill slope, and told Brittney how he felt about her. He told her how he'd felt as she was confiding in him in her tent, how he wished she'd look at him differently, and consider him as more than "a friend." He noticed that her eyes hardly ever left his as he spoke. Upon making their way to camp, Jason and Brittney stood facing each other in the middle of the dirt road that split the assemblage of tents in two.

"There," he said with finality. "I said it." He flashed a fearful smile at her.

She stepped close to him. He steeled himself for the "I really like you . . . as a friend" speech.

"Jason, you've been such a good friend to me. I have so much fun with you! You're always there for me when I need you, and you're the kind of guy any girl could love. But . . . "

Jason sighed and tried not to let his face reflect his hurt. "But what . . . ?" he asked.

"I just don't understand why you didn't say something sooner." Brittney said, with a mixture of regret and excitement. "I guess I just never thought you'd be interested. I always thought you just wanted to be my friend. I didn't think you could ever think of me as . . . "

Jason's eyes widened and he searched her face. Every muscle in his body seemed to stand at attention, like a new recruit at boot camp.

Brittney dropped her gaze from Jason's face and studied his shirt buttons. "I mean, you've always been the kind of guy I've needed and wanted for a long time . . . you know, a strong Christian, somebody with some character. I just never thought you'd go for me." She shrugged. "Especially not now. After Matt, I didn't think you'd want me."

Jason stared at Brittney, unbelieving, unspeaking. They faced each other in emotional silence. Finally, she lifted her face and smiled shyly.

"I wish you had told me all that a long time ago," she said.

Jason swallowed. "I do too," he said. They stared at each other for a long moment, until she reached her lips to his and kissed him lightly.

"Goodnight, Jason," she said. "See you in the morning."

The Inside Story: Whose Rules Rule?

Brittney got alone with God in a pretty dynamic way on that mountain! And she realized some important things about the decisions she'd been struggling with.

She saw that her struggle with right and wrong ultimately came down to a struggle between her way and God's way. The real issue was not, *What's right and what's wrong?* but *Whose version of right and wrong will I accept—my own or God's? Whose rules rule?*

CONSIDER THE CHOICE. God has revealed—in the Garden of Eden, on Mount Sinai, through Jesus Christ, in the words of Holy Scripture—absolute standards of right and wrong that reflect His nature. He has decreed honesty as right and dishonesty as wrong. He has decreed that sex within marriage is honorable, and sex outside of marriage is dishonorable. He has established justice as a virtue, and injustice as a vice.

You have many important choices to make in life, but the most important choice is whose version of right and wrong you will accept.

COMPARE IT TO GOD. The next step is to compare that attitude or action in question to what God has to say about it. It's not a matter of figuring out what's "right for me," it's a matter of determining who God is and what He has said about it.

Yet many of us—and our peers—feel uncomfortable with God's position on various matters. Our ways are not naturally the ways of God. So our tendency is to excuse and justify our way as the right way. But by doing so we are deceived into believing the wrong things are right and the right things are not for us.

When you decide to compare your attitudes and actions to God and what He says, you are acknowledging that God is God. You are saying that He is the Righteous Judge, that He alone defines and decides what things are right and what things are wrong . . . and He does that simply by being God. His nature defines right and wrong: those actions and attitudes that are not like Him are wrong. When you give up your imagined "rights" to determine right and wrong for yourself, you **ADMIT** that God is sovereign and He and He alone has that right.

COMMIT TO GOD'S WAY. Committing to God's way is easier said than done. First, as we just pointed out, it is uncomfortable to compare our ways to God's ways. It's never comfortable to admit we are wrong. That's why the concept of deciding what is "right for you" is so appealing— it permits us to justify our wrong attitudes and actions.

But, secondly, even when we do recognize our selfishness and sinfulness, committing to God's way in reality seems almost impossible. In fact, it is impossible to live out God's way in our own power. But God has promised to infuse us with His power to live according to His ways when we **SUBMIT** to Him as Savior and Lord of our lives.

The way to do this is:

1. *Turn from your selfish ways and confess your sin* (see 1 John 1:9). Turn (repent of your sin) by acknowledging that you have been living contrary to God's ways, that you have been trying to "do your own thing" and that you have been going your own way; you must agree that your own way is wrong. When you sincerely repent and turn your back on your sin, you can claim (trust) God's full and free forgiveness.

2. *Turn control of your life over to the Lord.* If God can keep planets spinning in space, rivers running to the seas, and seasons coming and going, do you think He will mess up your life if you give Him control? He can cleanse and satisfy your soul with His eyes closed, if you'll let Him. If you have not trusted God for salvation, a simple, heartfelt prayer such as the following one can open your life to the love and light of God:

> Lord Jesus, I want to know You personally. Thank You for dying on the cross for my sins. I open the door of my life and receive You as my Savior and Lord. Thank You for forgiving my sins and giving me eternal life. Take control of the throne of my life. Make me the kind of person You want me to be. Amen.

3. *Trust God to fill you and lead you by His Spirit.* God calls us to respond to His love by allowing Him to be Lord of our

lives and fill us with His Spirit. Being filled with the Spirit means that He is directing our lives and giving us His power to resist temptation, gain courage, make right choices, and deal with everything that happens in our lives each day. What must we do to be filled with the Holy One?

We must present every area of our lives to God (see Rom. 12:1-2). We must ask God to help us surrender every area of our lives to Him—activities, friends, desires, etc.—and tell Him we want to depend on Him to lead us in each area.

Next, we must ask the Holy Spirit to fill us. God commands us to be filled with the Holy Spirit (see Eph. 5:18). Asking to be filled is a clear step of obedience.

Finally, we must believe that He fills us when we ask Him to. The Holy Spirit is a free gift to be received. God has promised to answer if we pray and express our request to be filled (1 John 5:14-15).

Following is a suggested prayer expressing your desire to be filled with the Holy Spirit:

> Dear Father, I need You. I acknowledge that I have been in charge of my own life. I have sinned against You. Please forgive me. I thank You that You have forgiven my sins through Christ's death on the cross. Jesus, I ask You to take Your place on the throne of my life. Fill me with the Holy Spirit as You commanded me to be filled, and as You promised in Your Word that You would do if I asked in faith. Thank You for taking charge of my life and for filling me with the Holy Spirit.

4. Keep walking in the power of the Spirit. Trusting God to fill us with His Spirit doesn't mean that we will never again blow it through lack of faith or disobedience. But we can live more consistently day after day as we live in the power of God's Spirit.

And when we blow it, we must again confess our sin quickly and turn back to God. We must yield again to His Spirit and tell Him He is in control of our lives.

We must build our faith through the study of God's Word and through prayer (see Rom. 10:17).

And we must be prepared for spiritual conflict against the world (1 John 2:15-17), the flesh (Gal. 5:16-21), and Satan (1 Pet. 5:8-9), and respond to the conflict by relying on God's Spirit working in us and through us.

COUNT ON GOD'S PROTECTION AND PROVISION. When we humbly **ADMIT** God's sovereignty and sincerely **SUBMIT** to His loving authority, we can begin not only to see clearly the distinctions between right and wrong, but we can also see God's loving motivation. In this fourth step, we need to thank God for His protection and provision. This doesn't mean everything will be rosy; in fact, God's Word says that we may suffer for righteousness' sake. But such suffering has great rewards. Living according to God's way and allowing the Holy Spirit to live through us brings many spiritual blessings, like freedom from guilt, a clear conscience, the joy of sharing Christ, and most importantly the love and smile of God on our lives. Additionally, we enjoy many physical, emotional, psychological, and relational benefits when we are obedient to God. While God's protection and provision should not be our primary motivation to obey God, it certainly provides a powerful reinforcement for us to choose the right and reject the wrong.

12

The Aftermath

"Never," Maury shouted, "*never* has my division suffered a fallout like this!" He looked around him at the devastation: broken cables waved from the walls and ceiling like wounded snakes, wisps of black smoke arose from the computer console, multi-colored liquids oozed from shattered beakers and jars on the lab tables and floors, and a persistent hissing sound escaped from a broken hose that dangled from the ceiling.

Ratsbane, who had long ago lost his antennae in similar fallouts, emerged slowly from under the console. He struggled to his frog-like feet and raised his ant-head with effort.

"That *was* a bad one," he said, twisting his torso to crack his back. The fallout, created by the activity of Brittney's prayers had lasted a long time and caused considerable damage throughout the Research and Intelligence Division.

"Quick," Maury snapped. "Go out there," he said, pointing to the laboratory door that led to the other sections of RAID, "and find me a monitor that still works."

"What?" Ratsbane screeched.

"We still have a chance," Maury muttered. He crept behind the computer console and began separating damaged wires and components from those that had escaped damage.

"It's over!" Ratsbane croaked. "Can't you see that?"

"It ain't over till it's over," Maury responded as he twisted loose wires together. "Sure, she's submitted to the Sovereign Lord, and there's nothing we can do about that. But she hasn't told ol' graybeard yet; she still hasn't acted on the truth. That means there's still time. All I have to do is use the others to keep her from following through. Now get me what I need—and make it fast!"

"If you ask me," Ratsbane mumbled, "I think your strategy went down the Pit."

"Nobody's asking you," Maury snapped.

☆ ☆ ☆

Brittney arrived at the mess tent the next morning before any of the others. Darkness still enveloped the camp as she hurriedly made her breakfast and then sat down to wait.

Avi arrived a few minutes before four o'clock and immediately set to work in the kitchen. She chatted easily with Brittney, who helped her friend set food and utensils out on the table. Jason and Philip staggered in as the girls were finishing their preparations.

Brittney grabbed Avi's arm and pulled her to meet the boys just inside the door.

"I've got something really important to tell you guys," Brittney said, a mixture of urgency and mystery in her voice. She led the group to the corner table and sat down beside Jason, facing Philip and Avi.

"What's going on?" Jason asked, intrigued by Brittney's tone but uncertain whether to be excited or worried. Philip covered a wide yawn with a hand.

"Where's Bryan?" she asked.

"Bryan?" Jason echoed. "He said he wasn't coming to breakfast. I don't think he slept much last night. I guess Shebtai's taking him to the airport in a couple of hours. Why? What's this all about?"

Brittney inhaled deeply, and then slowly and methodically began to relate the story of Friday night. She told them how she had heard Susan Arens's voice on her way back from the water hole and how she had discovered Bryan, Susan, and the Land Rover. She explained how, when Bryan had been accused of vandalizing that Arab grocery, she had known he was innocent but was unwilling to speak up because of how her truthfulness would affect her.

"I've done a lot of thinking ever since the storm on the mountain," she said, speaking slowly and deliberately. "Darcelle and I stayed up together, and talked some things out. And I've begun to realize how I've been trying to figure things out and do things on my own. I've been pretty much ignoring God, and rejecting what He says is right, and trying to substitute my own version of what's right. She licked her lips nervously. But last night I guess I saw that I was just mainly being disobedient. I saw that what I really needed to do was just submit to Him and do what He says is right, not what I think is right.

"Now," she said, "I just have to tell Shebtai." She lowered her gaze and studied her hands, which were shaking. "I'll try not to get you guys in trouble," she said without looking up, "but I'm not going to lie anymore."

Jason stared at her, his eyes wide and his mouth open. "You've got two demerits, Brittney," he said.

"I know," she answered.

"What if he sends you home?" Philip asked.

Brittney looked at Jason, her eyes welling with tears. She dropped her gaze to her hands again, which were folded on the table in front of her, trembling. She screwed her lips shut to keep them from quivering.

Jason turned his body on the bench and faced Brittney. He leaned his left elbow on the table and gripped Brittney's upper arm with his right hand. "You can't!" he said.

She turned tearful eyes toward him. "I have to," she whispered.

"But . . . ," he gasped in frustration. "You *don't* have to."
He searched his mind for a way to say what he was thinking.
What about us? he wanted to say. *We just got started. We've got
almost four weeks left, Brittney, but if you tell Shebtai, you'll have
to go home. Then what chance will we have?*

But he said none of that. Instead, he placed his left hand
atop her interlocked fingers and continued to hold her arm
with his right hand. "Look, Brittney," he said, lowering his
voice. "Bryan's already packed. He's all ready to go. You
don't have to say anything."

She blinked at him, pain showing through her moist
eyes.

"He's been nothing but a pain to everybody, Brittney,"
Jason pleaded. "And now that he and Susan are broken up,
he probably wouldn't want to stay, anyway."

She closed her eyes.

"No, look at me, Brittney. Look at me!" he pleaded. She
opened her eyes. He stopped, and they stared at each other
with emotion-filled faces.

"It's not like anybody's asking you to lie," Philip said,
jumping into the conversation. "But you can't lie if you don't
say anything, can you?"

"That's what I've been telling myself all along," she
began, but Philip interrupted her before she could finish.

"And you were right," he said. "Look, don't you see
how great a summer this'll be if you just let things happen?
Me and Avi, you and Jason . . . we can have so much fun
together. You'd spoil everything by telling on yourself, not
just for you and Jason, but for me and Avi too."

Brittney closed her eyes briefly, and then opened them
to look around at her friends. She studied their faces and saw
their concern, not just for themselves, but for her too.

Avi reached a hand across the table and covered
Brittney's clasped hands. "I know you must do what you
think is right," Avi said, "but telling Father would not just
spoil things for us; it would hurt him too. He would be dis-

appointed in me, yes, but he would also be disappointed in you. He likes you, Brittney. It would hurt him to have to send you home."

Brittney scooted the bench back and stood, facing her friends. She wrestled with her emotions for a few moments before speaking.

"It's going to hurt me, too, Avi . . . I can't tell you how much," she said, and stopped. Her lip quivered. "But I don't have to do what's right for me. I have to do what God says is right. I wish I could explain it to you guys; I'm only just beginning to understand it myself, but I know God is true, and honest, and I know I haven't been. And that's why I've been wrong."

She walked slowly to the door of the mess tent and turned to face her friends again. They stared back at her as if she were marching off to her death.

The door shut behind her, and Philip, Avi, and Jason sat unmoving, as if they were chained to the table. No one spoke; they were all absorbed in their own thoughts.

Jason felt like someone had kicked him in the gut. He replayed the events of last night, and the heady optimism he had felt since those intoxicating moments. He recalled Brittney's words: "You're just the kind of guy I've been looking for, Jason—the kind of guy I've wanted and needed for a long time—a strong Christian, somebody with character." The words echoed in his ears. *I guess I didn't show much character this morning, did I? I pretty much told her she should lie to make me happy.* He focused his hazy eyes on Philip and Avi, who sat wordlessly watching him.

Yeah, that's a great way to begin a relationship. He kicked himself mentally. *If I expect her to lie for me, what makes me think she wouldn't someday lie to me?* He realized she could be thinking similar thoughts; if he would ask her to lie, could she trust him not to lie to her?

He blew a noisy blast of air through his lips, as if he were playing an invisible tuba. "Brittney's right," he told

Philip and Avi. "Whether she lies by what she says or what she doesn't say, it's all the same. She stood up to all three of us because she chose to do the right thing. I don't know about you two, but I think that's incredible." He stood. "And I can't believe I let her go to Shebtai by herself!" He started for the door.

"Jason," Avi called, scraping her and Philip's bench against the floor as she stood. "Wait. I'll come too."

"Wait a minute," Philip said. He still sat at the table, looking up at Jason and Avi. "What about me?"

"What about you?" Jason echoed.

"You're going with Brittney to tell Shebtai about the other night." It was a statement, not a question. "That means I pretty much have to go too."

"You don't have to," Jason said.

Philip rolled his eyes. His face registered disgust and frustration. Finally, he sighed in resignation, and stood. "Yes, I do," he said.

They walked through the door of the mess hall and were nearly run over by a speeding Jeep, which skidded to a stop, spraying dirt and rocks, in front of the mess tent.

The Israeli official who had brought the news of the vandalism in Mizpeh Ramon to the camp yesterday leaped from the Jeep and faced them with a fist planted on each hip. The Israeli soldier still sat behind the wheel of the Jeep.

"Where is Dr. Levitt?" the man barked. "I must see him. Now."

═══════════════════════════════════════

The Inside Story: A Daniel-like Stand

Many years ago, a young prince watched as his nation was conquered by a foreign army. The foreigners took him prisoner and carted him hundreds of miles away to a strange city, where he was ordered to be trained for the king's service. The prince was required to learn the language and literature of the conquering nation, and was served daily helpings of sumptuous food and wine.

However, the prince was a Jew, which meant that he observed strict rules about what he could eat, and how his food had to be prepared. He explained his predicament to his superior.

"I'd like to help you," the official said, "but it's my job to keep you strong and healthy; the king will have my head—literally—if you become weak or pale."

So the prince proposed a solution for him and the other Jews who were training for the king's service. "Do this," he said. "Give me and my buddies nothing but vegetables to eat and water to drink for ten days. Then compare our appearance with that of the young men who eat the royal food. If we don't look as healthy as they do, you can do whatever you want with us."

At the end of the trial period, the young prince and his friends looked healthier and better nourished than the men who feasted on ham and eggs. The prince and his friends not only stood firm for their convictions; they also quickly became the king's most valued advisors.

That young prince's name was Daniel, and his story was written down in the Old Testament book as the Book of Daniel. He was a trusted advisor of several kings, and his whole life was marked by a series of challenges in which he stood for truth in the face of great and dangerous opposition (which once included being thrown into a den of hungry lions).

Daniel took a stand for truth regardless of the cost. He determined to do the right thing because he was convinced that God's commands (which proceeded from His nature) were true. He was probably also aware that right choices would, in the long run, bring the greatest benefits.

Similarly, Brittney has finally come to recognize that, no matter how easy it appears to be, lying—whether by what she says or what she doesn't say—is a transgression of God's command, and a violation of the divine principle of honesty. She also knows that dishonesty is wrong because it contradicts and offends the very nature of God, who is true.

And, importantly, not only has she discerned what is right, she has decided to do it. But her dilemma at Har Karkom will certainly not be her last; Brittney, like all of us, will face daily choices between right and wrong. She will encounter daily challenges, daily opportunities to implement the "Four Cs"—**consider the choice, compare it to God, commit to God's way,** and **count on God's protection and provision.**

Standing for truth is not like getting braces or passing your SATs; you don't just do it once and forget about it. Standing for truth is a way of life, a whole new way of thinking and choosing. It's a day-by-day, minute-by-minute decision to **consider, compare, commit,** and **count on**. It's a whole new way to live in relationship with our Creator God.

That may seem pretty overwhelming, of course. After all, who follows the truth every day? Who does the right thing every minute? Nobody's perfect—except for Jesus, and He's the key to standing for truth. Remember, He said, "I am the way and the truth and the life" (John 14:6). The truth is alive! If you have trusted Jesus Christ as Savior and Lord, you have the Truth living inside you. Because, as we have said, standing for truth isn't about rules; it's about relationship . . . a personal relationship with (and constant dependence on) the Truth Himself!

To help you on your incredible journey to make right choices, we have created a *Right from Wrong Workbook* called *Setting You Free to Make Right Choices*. Take twenty minutes a day with yourself, God, and your *Right from Wrong Workbook* and discover a new way of thinking, a new way of relating to God, and a new way of making choices in life. Talk to your youth group leader about the *Setting You Free to Make Right Choices* workbook and get your entire youth group involved. The *Right from Wrong Workbooks* are available in Christian bookstores, published by Broadman and Holman Publishers.

I challenge you to never again think of the commands of God as "dos and don'ts," "shalls and shall nots." See them as God's way to reveal His very nature and character to you and through you. See them as God's loving desire to protect you and provide for you. Take a stand for truth, let the Truth live in you, and share the Truth with others.

13

Brittney's Last Stand

Brittney stood before Shebtai's tent as the morning sun poked its first tentative fingers into the eastern sky. The dig director wore jeans and a short-sleeve shirt.

Brittney recounted her story to Shebtai without mentioning Philip, Avi, and Jason by name, though she realized that he would certainly know who had accompanied her to the water hole Friday evening. She also explained that she had not said anything before because of her demerit situation, and related in great detail how the storm on the mountain had caused her change of heart.

Shebtai's face clouded with increasing sadness as he listened to Brittney's recitation. The corners of his eyes crinkled with anguish. "I—I find this so hard to believe," he said when she had finished. "You're not just making this up to protect Bryan, are you?"

She shook her head.

"No, I didn't think so," Shebtai said sadly. "Well, you know, the authorities are going to need more than that." He paused. "Are you prepared to tell them who was with you that night?"

Jason's voice answered Shebtai's question, as he and Philip and Avi arrived upon the scene. "She doesn't have to," he said. "Because we're the ones she went swimming with." Jason strode to Brittney's side and draped a friendly arm around her shoulder. Philip and Avi stood behind her, holding hands.

"Dr. Levitt!" bellowed the Israeli official, who had followed Brittney's friends. "I must speak to you."

Shebtai lifted his gaze beyond Brittney and the others and glanced briefly at the man. "In a moment," he answered, returning his gaze to Brittney. "It is true, then," he said to her.

"Dr. Levitt!" the curly-haired man repeated.

"In a moment, I said." His voice was quiet, but sharp. "Brittney," he said, extending his hand beneath her chin as if he were about to give her a chin-chuck. He spoke while holding her chin between his thumb and forefinger. "I want to be sure you understand what you are saying. You have two demerits already."

"Yes," Brittney answered in a whisper. Her forehead wrinkled and she forced her lips together.

The creases at the corners of his eyes deepened. "I am so sorry," he said. "I am so sorry." He withdrew his large hand from her petite chin. "I wish there were something I could do."

Brittney nodded without taking her eyes from Shebtai's face. "I know," she whispered.

"Dr. Levitt!" the official repeated. "I must insist—"

"What is it?" Shebtai answered firmly.

"The young American does not have to leave. There is new information that clears him completely." He fished his sunglasses out of his shirt pocket and placed them on his face, though the sun had peeked over the horizon just moments before. "You have a volunteer by the name of David?" he asked, pronouncing the name Da-veed. "An Ethiopian Jew?"

Shebtai flashed a quick look at Brittney, then at the others. An ironic smile tugged the corners of his mouth. He nodded.

"I must place him under arrest," the man in the sunglasses said.

☆   ☆   ☆

Maury turned his spectacled face away from the twelve-inch monochrome monitor on which he had been working and glared at Ratsbane.

"I hold you personally responsible," Maury squawked. "It's all your fault!"

"My fault?" Ratsbane sneered. "How is it my fault? I wasn't even near the controls when the girl stood up to her friends. I wasn't working the keyboard when she told the old man the truth! And I had absolutely nothing to do with the others' decisions to back her up! It was *your* stinking strategy that caused all this," he said, pointing around him at the ruined laboratory. "You can't blame *me!*"

Maury rapped the side of Ratsbane's head. "Yes, I can! Because you let her come to understand what makes things right or wrong . . . no, more importantly, who it is that decides those things. You let ol' graybeard carry on about the Enemy and the Law. If it weren't for you, I could have kept her from submitting to the Enemy and from influencing her friends with her new-found integrity!

"Do you understand what you have done? Do you even suspect what those kids can do if they begin to understand the Person of Truth and begin to take a stand in front of their friends and families? Do you know where we'll be if they all begin to admit the moral authority of the Sovereign Lord of the Universe—and submit their own will to His? *Do you?*" Maury was suddenly distracted by a commotion at the locked entrance to the RAID lab. He turned his head in time to see two gargantuan demons, each with the torso of a gorilla and the horned head of a rhinoceros, bash down the door with their thick forearms. They stomped on the fallen door and faced Maury and Ratsbane, panting loudly and waving their leathery paws wildly at the cloud of dust their entrance had stirred.

Ratsbane slapped Maury's turtle head, sending his superior's glasses flying to the floor. Maury turned his attention once more to Ratsbane—only now the demon with the ant-head became the aggressor.

"You arrogant little twerp!" He shouted at the director of RAID. "Nerdbrain! Nerdmeister! Nerd-o-rama!

Nerd-o-matic! Nerd-it-through-the-grapevine!" Ratsbane, who was the taller demon, leaned over Maury and began backing him to the wall.

"You think you know so much, don't you?" he shouted, as the gorilla-rhinos watched and waited. "You think you're this great genius, don't you? Well, I've got news for you: you're busted! These two demon brutes just heard you refer to the Enemy in unapproved terms." He pointed to the two beasts, whose mangy stench now filled the laboratory; they both waved tiny listening devices they gripped in their paws.

Maury looked from Ratsbane to the brutes, then back again. "You bugged my laboratory?" His voice rose in pitch to a pathetic whine.

"That's right, you little nerd from hell," Ratsbane admitted in menacing tones, as he reached under the console and extracted a device the size of a cigarette lighter. He waved the small transmitter cruelly in Maury's face.

The gorilla-rhino brutes gripped Maury by his arms and lifted his turtle form off the floor. His feet swung helplessly in the air.

"You can't do this!" he screamed. Without his round glasses, his turtle eyes squinted at Ratsbane. "You sabotaged my whole strategy, didn't you? You purposely neglected those bratty Westcastle kids, didn't you? You wanted the strategy to fail so you could take over RAID, didn't you?"

"Get him out of here," Ratsbane snarled. He stared after the brutes and their prisoner long after they had disappeared through the door. "You're wrong, nerdbrain," he whispered bitterly to himself. "I didn't defeat your strategy. The kids did it themselves; I just waited around patiently to cash in on the results!" He tossed the listening device onto the floor and crushed it under his webbed foot. Bugging each other's environments was not uncommon to hell's demonic forces. Teamwork was merely reserved for times when the independent approach was not possible;

most of the time in hell, however, it was every demon for himself. Just thinking about how well the kids' choices had played into his own devious schemes, Ratsbane chuckled with demonic glee. Then he lifted his dust-covered ant-head and peered around him with his obsidian eyes, assessing the day's damages.

"I've got a lot of cleaning up to do around here," he said, his voice echoing off the empty laboratory's ravaged walls.

☆   ☆   ☆

Brittney stood tearfully beside the Land Rover as Shebtai hefted her luggage into the rear of the vehicle. She had been at Har Karkom less than three weeks, but time had flown by, and she had done and learned so much.

She turned to Avi and hugged her Israeli friend tightly.

"I'll be seeing these guys in just over a month," she said through sniffs and sobs. "But I don't know when I'll ever see you again." They hugged tightly.

"We will keep in touch," Avi, who was also crying, said. "Father has talked about going to the United States for a long time. Maybe we can come to Westcastle sometime, and we will see each other again." "Brittney." A voice behind her quietly spoke her name.

She released her grip on Avi and turned around. Philip stood close to her, holding something in his hands.

"Here," he said. He placed twin objects in her upturned palms.

She looked down. He had given her the tiny liquor bottles he had stolen from the plane. She flashed him a puzzled, almost disgusted look. Was this his idea of a joke?

"I never planned to drink them or anything," he whispered. "I don't even like the stuff."

"What do you expect *me* to do with them?" she asked.

He shrugged. "I thought you could maybe just return them for me."

She smiled, and tucked the bottles into her pocket.

They hugged briefly then, and Brittney noticed as she looked over Philip's shoulder that Bryan had joined the group.

"I just wanted to say thanks," he said, without smiling. He cleared his throat. "For what you did." His gaze flitted from his shoes to her face, and back again.

"You don't have to thank me, Bryan," she said. "I should have told the truth yesterday. I'm sorry I took so long." A feeling of relief overwhelmed her; she knew without a doubt at that moment that if she had let Bryan leave Har Karkom and return home, she would have been unspeakably miserable for the rest of their trip.

She smiled through her tears and stepped forward to hug Bryan.

Shebtai started the Land Rover's engine. She jumped slightly with the sudden realization that it was time to go. She looked at Jason; the light of the morning sun glistened off his stubby blond hair, and he seemed much taller than before. Her eyes began to fill with tears, but she blinked them back. She smiled and threw her arms around his neck.

"I wish you didn't have to go," Jason said.

"Me too," she answered. She leaned backward slightly and looked into his blue eyes. They locked gazes as if they were reading each other's minds. Finally, she leaned her head forward again and kissed him. "Hurry home, Jason," she said softly, and her parting smile filled Jason's chest with a sweet, hopeful ache.

Moments later, she and Shebtai bounced down the rock-and-dirt path from Har Karkom to the two-lane highway that would lead them through Mizpeh Ramon and Beer Sheba to Ben Gurion International Airport in Tel Aviv.

Brittney and Shebtai rode for miles over the uneven road without speaking. She stared through the dusty windshield of the vehicle and reflected on her decision to tell the truth, and on the strange events that prompted her to submit to God, not only as the Judge of right and wrong, but also as the ultimate authority in all the choices she would make in her life. She remembered her mother, Penny Marsh, trying to help her realize that a thing is wrong if it contradicts or offends the nature of God Himself. She remembered her mother saying, several times, "God is the standard, Brittney." She told Brittney repeatedly that she must measure her actions—and herself—against Him, not against some self-conceived idea of right and wrong.

I thought I knew all that when I came to Har Karkom, she said to herself. *But it took a storm on the mountain to really make me understand that God gave His law—His whole Word, His whole revelation, even in Christ—not only so we could know right from wrong, but so we could know Him, because He's the Source of it all anyway.*

The Land Rover hit a bump that lifted Brittney into the air and dropped her back onto her seat with a rude thump. Shebtai threw her an apologetic look, but she remained engrossed in her own thoughts.

And the reason He wants me to know Him is so I can obey Him. She shook her head. *No, not just that. So He can bless me.* She smiled with satisfaction. *Yeah, because He loves me.*

She turned around in her seat and gazed back at the receding form of Har Karkom, which now appeared little larger than the rolling hills around Westcastle.

As she turned around, Brittney saw the ribbon of paved road stretching in front of them. A few minutes later, Shebtai pulled the Land Rover onto the pavement and turned north.

"You never answered Darcelle's question," Brittney said suddenly.

Shebtai's expression did not change. "What question is that?"

"Do you think Har Karkom is really Mount Sinai, where Moses actually met God and received the Ten Commandments?" She almost added, *and hid in the cleft of the rock?*

He paused so long that Brittney was afraid he had not heard her question, or perhaps had been angered by it. He finally spoke, however, without taking his eyes off of the road.

"I don't know," he said. He sighed. "Why do you ask?"

Brittney remembered standing on the edge of the mount and looking out over the plains below, imagining the tents of the Israelites spreading for miles. She mused on the fact that she had come down from that mountain last night with the precepts of God, not on stone tablets as Moses had, but engraved on her heart. She shrugged.

"It would be neat if it was," she said.

"It would be the find of the century," Shebtai answered seriously.

The Land Rover passed a large brown truck heading the opposite way, crammed with Israeli soldiers wearing brown khaki and matching berets.

Shebtai cleared his throat. "David confessed to his crime this morning."

Brittney heard what he said, but it took her a moment to realize he was speaking about the young Jew who did the things Bryan had been accused of doing.

"It seems young David has some rather extreme views about Arabs in Israel. Someone from Mizpeh Ramon finally identified him to the authorities."

Brittney nodded. A wry smile crossed her face. If she could have just kept quiet another five minutes or so, Bryan would have been cleared anyway.

"I am very sorry these things affected you the way they did," Shebtai said.

Brittney leaned her head against the back of the seat and turned her face toward Shebtai. "Don't be sorry," she said. A smile spread slowly across her face. "I'm not. I'm not sorry at all."

Additional Resources

To obtain a free catalog of Josh McDowell resources that includes the latest Right from Wrong Campaign products write:

Josh McDowell Ministry
P. O. Box 1000 C
Dallas, Texas 75221

Resources for Youth

BOOKS

The Love Killer—The PowerLink Chronicles by Josh McDowell and Bob Hostetler—Word, Inc.

Under Siege—The PowerLink Chronicles by Josh McDowell and Chuck Klein—Word, Inc.

Don't Check Your Brains at the Door by Josh McDowell and Bob Hostetler—Word, Inc.

The Teenage Q & A Book by Josh McDowell and Bill Jones—Word, Inc.

Thirteen Things You Gotta Know to Make It as a Christian (devotional) by Josh McDowell and Bob Hostetler—Word, Inc.

Thirteen Things You Gotta Know to Keep Your Love Life Alive and Well (devotional) by Josh McDowell and Bob Hostetler—Word, Inc.

WORKBOOKS

The Right from Wrong Workbook—Setting You Free to Make Right Choices (Junior/Senior High Edition) by Josh McDowell—Broadman & Holman Publishers

The Right from Wrong Workbook—The Moral Maze (college edition) by Josh McDowell—Broadman & Holman Publishers

The Right from Wrong Workbook—Truth Works (younger children's edition and older children's edition) by Josh McDowell—Broadman & Holman Publishers

VIDEO SERIES FOR JUNIOR/SENIOR HIGH STUDENTS

"Setting You Free to Make Right Choices" Right from Wrong Video Series by Josh McDowell—Word, Inc.

"See You at the Party" Video Series by Josh McDowell—Word, Inc.

"Won by One" Audio and Video Series by Josh McDowell and Dann Spader—Word, Inc.

"Don't Check Your Brains at the Door" Video Series by Josh McDowell—Word, Inc.

Revised "No—The Positive Answer" by Josh McDowell—Word, Inc.

"Teenage Q & A" Video Series by Josh McDowell—Word, Inc.

Resources for Adults

BOOKS

Right from Wrong—What You Need to Know to Help Youth Make Right Choices by Josh McDowell and Bob Hostetler—Word, Inc.

How to Be a Hero to Your Kids by Josh McDowell and Dick Day—Word, Inc.

Why Wait?—What You Need to Know About the Teen Sexuality Crisis by Josh McDowell and Dick Day—Thomas Nelson Publishers

How to Help Your Child Say No to Sexual Pressure by Josh McDowell—Word, Inc.

WORKBOOKS

The Right from Wrong Workbook—Truth Matters (adult edition) by Josh McDowell—Broadman & Holman Publishers

AUDIO

Right from Wrong Book on Tape by Josh McDowell—Word, Inc.

VIDEO SERIES FOR ADULTS

"The Right from Wrong—Truth Matters" Video Series for Adults by Josh McDowell—Word, Inc.

"How to Be a Hero to Your Kids" Video Series by Josh McDowell—Word, Inc.

"How to Help Your Child Say No to Sexual Pressure" Video Series by Josh McDowell—Word, Inc.

"Let's Talk About Love and Sex" Video Pack for home use by Josh McDowell—Word, Inc.

About the Authors

Josh McDowell is an internationally known speaker, author, and traveling representative for Campus Crusade for Christ. A graduate of Wheaton College and Talbot Theological Seminary, he has written more than thirty-five books and appeared in numerous films, videos, and television series. He and his wife, Dottie, live in Julian, California, with their four children.

Bob Hostetler is a writer, editor, and speaker. He has written seven books, including *Don't Check Your Brains at the Door, The Love Killer* (both co-authored with Josh McDowell), and *They Call Me A.W.O.L.*

He and his wife, Robin, live in southwestern Ohio with their two children, Aubrey and Aaron.

Passing on the Truth to Our Next Generation

The "Right From Wrong" message, available in numerous formats, provides a blueprint for countering the culture and rebuilding the crumbling foundations of our families.

Read It and Embrace a New Way of Thinking

The Right From Wrong Book to Adults

Right From Wrong - What You Need to Know to Help Youth Make Right Choices
by Josh McDowell & Bob Hostetler

Our youth no longer live in a culture that teaches an objective standard of right and wrong. Truth has become a matter of taste. Morality has been replaced by individual preference. And today's youth have been affected. Fifty-seven percent (57%) of our churched youth cannot state that an objective standard of right and wrong even exists!

As the centerpiece of the "Right From Wrong" Campaign, this life-changing book provides you with a biblical, yet practical, blueprint for passing on core Christian values to the next generation.

Right From Wrong, Tradepaper Book
ISBN 0-8499-3604-7

The Truth Slayers Book to Youth

The Truth Slayers - A Battle of Right From Wrong
by Josh McDowell & Bob Hostetler

This book–directed to youth–is written in the popular NovelPlus format and combines the fascinating story of Brittney Marsh, Philip Milford and Jason Withers and the consequences of their wrong choices with Josh McDowell's insights for young adults in sections called "The Inside Story."

The Truth Slayers conveys the critical "Right From Wrong" message that challenges you to rely on God's word as the absolute standard of truth in making right choices.

The Truth Slayers, Tradepaper Book
ISBN 0-8499-3662-4

Hear It and Adopt a New Way of Teaching

Right From Wrong Audio for Adults
by Josh McDowell

What is truth? In three powerful and persuasive talks based on the book *Right From Wrong*, Josh McDowell provides you, your family, and the church with a sound, thorough, biblical, and workable method to clearly understand and defend the truth. Josh explains how to identify absolutes and shows you how to teach youth to determine what is absolutely right from wrong.

Right From Wrong, Audio–104
ISBN 0-8499-6195-5

See It and Commit to a New Way of Living

Video Series to Adults

Truth Matters for You and Tomorrow's Generation
Five-part Video Series featuring Josh McDowell

Josh McDowell is at his best in this hard-hitting series that goes beyond surface answers and quick fixes to tackle the real crisis of truth. You will discover the reason for this crisis, and more importantly, how to get you and your family back on track. This series is directed to the entire adult community and is excellent for building momentum in your church to address the loss of values within the family.

This series includes five video sessions, a comprehensive Leader's Guide including samplers from the five "Right From Wrong" Workbooks, the *Right From Wrong* book, the *The Truth Slayers* book, and a 12-minute promotional video tape to motivate adults to go through the series.

Truth Matters, Adult Video Series
ISBN 0-8499-8587-0

Video Series to Youth

Setting You Free to Make Right Choices
Five-part Video Series featuring Josh McDowell

Through captivating video illustrations, dynamic teaching sessions, and creative group interaction, this series presents students with convincing evidence that right moral choices must be based on a standard outside of themselves. This powerful course equips your students with the understanding of what is right from what is wrong.

The series includes five video sessions, Leader's Guide with reproducible handout including samplers from the five "Right From Wrong" Workbooks, and the *The Truth Slayers* book.

*Setting You Free to Make
Right Choices*, Youth Video Series
ISBN 0-8499-8585-4

Practice It and Make Living the Truth a Habit

Workbook for Adults
Truth Matters for You and Tomorrow's Generation
Workbook by Josh McDowell with Leader's Guide

The "Truth Matters" Workbook includes 35 daily activities that help you to instill within your children and youth such biblical values as honesty, love, and sexual purity. By taking just 25 - 30 minutes each day, you will discover a fresh and effective way to teach your family how to make right choices—even in tough situations.

The "Truth Matters" Workbook is designed to be used in eight adult group sessions that encourage interaction and support building. The five daily activities between each group meeting will help you and your family make right choices a habit.

Truth Matters, Member's Workbook ISBN 0-8054-9834-6
Truth Matters, Leader's Guide ISBN 0-8054-9833-8

Workbook for College Students
Out of the Moral Maze
by Josh McDowell with Leader's Instructions

Students entering college face a culture that has lost absolutes. In today's society, truth is a matter of taste; individual preference. "Out of the Moral Maze" will truth-seeking collegiate with a sound moral guidance based on God and His Word as the determining factc for making right moral choices.

Out of the Moral Maze, Member's Workbook wit
Leader's Instructions
ISBN 0-8054-9832-X

Workbook for Junior High and High School Students

Setting You Free to Make Right Choices
by Josh McDowell with Leader's Guide

With a Bible-based emphasis, this Workbook creatively and systematically teaches your students how to determine right from wrong in their everyday lives—specifically applying the decision-making process to moral questions about lying, cheating, getting even, and premarital sex.

Through eight youth group meetings followed each week with five daily exercises of 20-25 minutes per day, your teenagers will be challenged to develop a life-long habit of making right moral choices.

Setting You Free to Make Right Choices, Member's Workbook
ISBN 0-8054-9828-1
Setting You Free to Make Right Choices, Leader's Guide
ISBN 0-8054-9829-X

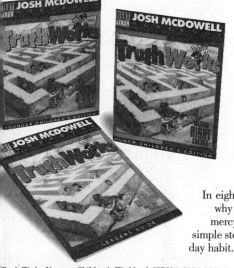

Workbook for Children

Truth Works - Making Right Choices
by Josh McDowell with Leader's Guide

To pass on the truth and reclaim a generation, we must teach God's truth when our children's minds and hearts are young and pliable. Creatively developed, "Truth Works" is two workbooks, one directed to younger children grades 1 - 3 and one to older children grades 4 - 6.

In eight fun-filled group sessions, your children will discover why such truths as honesty, justice, love, purity, self-control, mercy, and respect work to their best interests and how four simple steps will help them to make right moral choices an everyday habit.

Truth Works, Younger Children's Workbook ISBN 0-8054-9831-1
Truth Works, Older Children's Workbook ISBN 0-8054-9830-3
Truth Works, Leader's Guide ISBN 0-8054-9827-3

Contact your Christian supplier to help you obtain these "Right From Wrong" resources and begin to make it right in your home, your church, and your community.